FINDING PRINCE CHARMING

After a disastrous first night, Eleanor abandons London's West End for her grandparents' home in the Scottish Highlands. But her plans to lie low are foiled when she's asked to save the village panto. With an old flame waiting in the wings, some real-life Ugly Sisters making mischief, and a Hollywood star setting her pulse racing, Eleanor finds more than she bargained for in not-so-sleepy Tullymuir. Will she also find her Prince Charming and get the happy ending she deserves?

VICTORIA GARLAND

FINDING PRINCE CHARMING

Complete and Unabridged

LINFORD
Leicester

First published in Great Britain in 2019

First Linford Edition
published 2020

A catalogue record for this book is available
from the British Library.

ISBN 978–1–4448–4614–0

Published by
Ulverscroft Limited
Anstey, Leicestershire

Set by Words & Graphics Ltd.
Anstey, Leicestershire
Printed and bound in Great Britain by
TJ Books Limited, Padstow, Cornwall

This book is printed on acid-free paper

1

Well, that was that, then! Eleanor managed to get into the taxi and give the cabbie her address before she broke down and sobbed. All her dreams had come to nothing — all her hard work had been a complete waste of time.

'Are you all right, love?' the cabbie asked, his eyes full of concern in the rear-view mirror.

'Not really,' Eleanor managed to gasp out between sobs. 'What gave me away?' she asked with a weak chuckle.

'That's the ticket, love! You look on the bright side. At least you haven't lost your sense of humour. And I can tell you right now — whoever he was, he definitely isn't worth breaking your heart over. There's plenty more fish in the sea. A pretty girl like you will soon find someone else.'

At any other time, Eleanor might

have been annoyed by the cabbie's assumption that she was crying over a failed romance, but tonight she was just grateful for his kindness and concern.

If only it was as simple as breaking up with a boyfriend, which was painful at the time, but something everyone had been through and survived. But the end of what had been a very promising career? That was going to be a whole lot harder to bounce back from.

When the taxi dropped her home, Eleanor closed the front door and leaned against it with relief. It was wonderful to shut the world outside. She shrugged off her faux fur coat, kicked off her high heels and sat down heavily on the communal stairs leading up to her first floor flat. As she rootled in her sparkly evening bag for her mobile phone she could hear the taxi pull away. That lovely cabbie must have waited to make sure she'd got safely inside before he left — bless him. She was glad she'd given him a decent tip.

Eleanor resumed her search. If her

phone was there, she should be able to feel it; she'd treated herself to a fancy cover dotted with Swarovski crystals and pearls when she'd landed her first ever job as a director.

Back then, *Heavens Above!* had seemed like a gift of a play for her debut, something light and humorous but with real heart and a serious message hidden in its froth. But tonight, the title just mocked her. *Heavens Above!* just about summed up tonight's opening performance.

Eleanor rummaged in the pockets of her coat half-heartedly. Suddenly she was overcome with tiredness. She abandoned the search, gathered her belongings and dragged herself upstairs. The adrenaline that had kept her going until now seemed to have drained away.

When she was safely inside her flat, she unzipped her black, sequinned dress and let the shiny fabric slither onto the floor at her feet. Without it, she felt lighter, free from constraint, able to breathe again. She emptied the contents of her bag onto the bed. Her phone definitely wasn't there.

She remembered turning it to aeroplane mode just before the show started so it wouldn't ring and bleep and buzz during the performance.

As if that could have made it any worse! The show had been a complete disaster from start to finish. And now, to top everything off, she'd lost her phone. Well, she certainly wouldn't be going back to the theatre to find it. She'd just have to get another one.

She went into the hall and picked up the landline she kept for emergencies. This definitely counted as an emergency.

'So, how did it go?' Eleanor's friend Susie asked eagerly when she picked up.

Eleanor tried to speak, but the words couldn't get past the aching lump in her throat. Hearing her friend's voice just made her cry again.

'Shh, shh,' Susie soothed. 'It'll be

OK, Ella. I'm sure it wasn't as bad as you think.'

'Worse,' Eleanor said gruffly.

'Come on, now. Take a deep breath and tell me exactly what happened.'

Eleanor blew her nose and sat down on the floor. 'I don't know where to start. There was all the usual pre-show chaos: props going missing, costumes which were fine in the dress rehearsal no longer fitting, Alan tinkering with the lighting rig at the last minute, microphones not working.'

'Same old, same old,' Susie commented.

'Exactly. That's what I thought,' Eleanor carried on. 'Then when the show starts the nerves vanish, all the hard work pays off and everyone puts in an amazing performance, right?'

'That's what usually happens, yes,' Susie agreed, hesitantly.

'Well, not tonight. Everything that could go wrong did go wrong — and more besides. People missed their cues, forgot their lines, stood in the wrong

5

places and then Brandon Stone put the tin lid on it by falling off the stage into the orchestra pit! He was OK — in fact, he was so drunk he wasn't even hurt. The idiot decided to have a few drinks to calm his nerves and got carried away.'

'Oh my goodness, he actually fell off the stage?' Susie asked, trying to stifle a giggle. 'I did try and tell you it was a mistake to put a Hollywood movie star in your first production. They're unpredictable and don't think the usual rules apply to them.'

'I know, I know,' Eleanor sighed. 'I just thought it would do us both a favour. Brandon wanted to have a go at theatre, so a small show like *Heavens Above!* off West End seemed like a good place for him to start. And I hoped his name might raise the profile of the first play I've directed professionally.'

'Well, it'll definitely have done that!' Susie exclaimed. 'Sorry, that wasn't helpful.'

'No, it wasn't,' Eleanor agreed.

'But you can't say I didn't warn you.'

'That's not helpful either!' Eleanor snapped. 'And yes, you were right. Brandon struggled from the very start. He's really not a very good actor at all. He's got the looks and the smouldering charm, but he couldn't get his head around the idea that in the theatre you can't just go back for another take and another until you get it right.'

'That's the problem with Hollywood movie stars. A lot of them really can't act. But I'm sorry you had to learn that the hard way,' Susie said.

'I'll never have anything to do with a Hollywood movie star again as long as I live.'

'At least *Heavens Above!* lived up to its name.'

Eleanor groaned. 'It's done that all right.' She knew her friend was only trying to make her laugh.

'So what will you do now?' Susie asked.

'I'm thinking about visiting my grandparents for a while, just until the

7

heat dies down a bit.'

'Don't they live in the wilds of Scotland?'

'I'd hardly call Tullymuir the wilds . . . '

'What? You're running away? How can you keep an eye on the play from hundreds of miles away?' Susie asked incredulously.

'I don't want to keep an eye on it! I want to get as far away as possible so I won't have to read all the terrible reviews. They probably don't get the London papers in Tullymuir and hopefully it won't make it into any of the tabloids. They'd have a field day writing about the jumped-up actress who thought she could direct a play.' She hugged her knees to her chest. 'It's my name that's going to be dragged through the mud, you know. Well, probably Brandon's too, but I don't have much sympathy for him — if he hadn't been legless, it wouldn't have been such a total disaster. Anyway, you know as well as I do that when opening night is over, the director's job is done.'

'You're not on Broadway! There's no associate director to take over,' Susie pointed out.

'No, but Marcus is a very experienced stage manager. He'll keep me posted and tell me if he needs me to come back for any reason. And we both know the cast are always happier without the director breathing down their necks, so maybe things will settle down when I'm not there. I've been totally stressed out the past few weeks and that's probably rubbed off on the actors.'

'I suppose you do deserve a break after all your hard work. I'm sorry it's turned out this way.'

'Me too. Maybe I'll just go back to acting. I don't think I'm cut out to be a director after all.'

'I wouldn't rush into a decision when you're feeling like this,' Susie advised. 'Why don't you take it easy for a bit? It's not that long until Christmas. You could come back in the New Year and make a fresh start.'

'I'll see,' Eleanor said, not wanting to commit herself. Right now she felt like hibernating for at least six months and preferably never showing her face in London again.

2

Eleanor had been lucky to get a seat on a direct flight from Gatwick to Inverness, leaving the next evening. She hadn't bothered packing much. Over the years, she'd stayed with her grandparents so often she had her own room in their house, complete with a wardrobe stuffed with plenty of her old clothes.

Thankfully, fashion wasn't a major issue in Tullymuir so if the jeans, blouses and jumpers lurking in the wardrobe weren't the latest style it wasn't a problem.

Tullymuir was a village in the Western Highlands which didn't attract many tourists. When she was younger this had annoyed Eleanor, who found its picturesque beauty and quiet charm far more appealing than that of its more showy neighbours with their clusters of

B&Bs and excessive numbers of gift shops selling tacky souvenirs.

It was only when she was older Eleanor realised why the place wasn't a tourist magnet. It was simple really: her grandparents' village wasn't located on the banks of a brooding loch, it nestled in a rugged glen, which the main roads completely by passed. It was what people referred to as 'off the beaten track'.

It couldn't even be found using a sat nav, so that effectively kept most of the tourists away. People only came across Tullymuir by accident, usually when they got lost on their way to somewhere else. It might as well have been a desert island, which in her current mood suited Eleanor down to the ground.

As she wandered round Gatwick's North Terminal, Eleanor was glad not to be battling with a trolley-load of luggage. The self-service check-in kept the queues moving, so she was surprised to see a crowd starting to develop in one particular corner of the concourse.

She watched for a moment to see what was going on. Suddenly a man detached himself from the throng and shot past at high speed. A few women raced after him and she wondered if he'd stolen someone's handbag until she noticed a pen and paper in one of the women's hands.

Oh, so he was obviously some kind of celebrity — that would explain the hat and sunglasses indoors. Eleanor wasn't much interested. Working evenings, as people in the theatre do, she didn't get much opportunity to watch television. The chances were it would be a 'celebrity' she wouldn't even recognise.

Later, she was standing staring at a pair of shoes in a shop window when someone bumped into her. She cried out, more in surprise than pain, and the person stopped to apologise. It was him again — the incognito celebrity.

'I'm terribly sorry,' he said, in a soft Scottish accent while flashing a hundred-watt smile at her. 'Are you all right?'

He barely seemed to register her reply, being too busy shooting furtive glances over his shoulder to see if he was being followed. Before she had time to tell him that he seemed to have shaken off his admirers, he was gone.

Eleanor wondered vaguely who the man was. There was something familiar about the smile, but not when combined with the accent. Maybe he wasn't an actor at all; he could be a rock star. Eleanor started to run through bands in her head, but she was none the wiser.

She bought a magazine to while away the time and forgot all about the stranger. Her heart started to sink when she checked the departure boards at regular intervals over the next half-hour and noticed more and more of the Scottish flights being delayed. It looked as if she was in for a long evening.

She found a quiet corner to sit and wait, buying a coffee to try and keep herself awake. But the caffeine only worked for so long and then Eleanor felt her eyes closing. She gave in. Last time she'd looked her flight time had been pushed back by an hour, so she'd have time for a quick snooze.

* * *

A short while later, she was woken abruptly by a weight on her legs and the sound of very clearly enunciated swearing. A man was sprawled on the floor beside her, his legs tangled up with hers. She quickly sat up, pulling her legs in and trying to work out what was going on.

'It's a bit late for that!' a deep voice growled, as the man got to his feet, rubbing his shin. 'Maybe next time you could keep your legs under control.'

'I was asleep,' she retorted. 'I can hardly be held responsible for what my legs do while I'm sleeping.' Seeing who it was, she added, 'And maybe if you spent more time looking where you're going instead of running away from

15

your fans, you wouldn't keep crashing into people.'

'Oh. Hello again. I suppose that's a fair point,' the man added, smiling sheepishly.

He sat down on the seat next to her and took off his hat and shades, running his hands through his light brown hair. His gorgeous blue eyes sparkled with humour. With the hat off, he looked even more familiar. But from where?

'Can't you just sign a few autographs so they'll leave you in peace?' Eleanor suggested.

'You're joking?' His eyebrows furrowed into a frown and his smile disappeared. 'You obviously have no idea how tenacious fans can be. A quick signature or even a selfie with me might satisfy some of them, but others can be really scary. One woman actually followed me into the gents' toilet earlier on!'

'Seriously?' Eleanor asked incredulously, trying unsuccessfully to stifle a giggle.

'Oh aye, it's really funny,' the man growled, 'unless of course it's happening to you. Then it becomes a lot less funny and a lot more like Meryl Streep in *Fatal Attraction*.'

'I'm sure your pet bunny is quite safe.'

'Only because I don't have one! You'd be horrified if you knew the lengths some people go to to try and attract my attention.'

Eleanor flushed. She hoped he didn't think she was one of those people. He probably thought she'd deliberately tripped him. That really annoyed her, especially as she still hadn't a clue who he was! Though something was stirring in her memory.

'I'm sorry, that sounded really big-headed and I hate people like that, don't you? All *look at me, aren't I wonderful*. It's just that being in the public eye isn't all it's cracked up to be sometimes.'

He gave another of his shy smiles, which Eleanor was finding difficult to resist. She decided to give him another chance.

They chatted for a while and Eleanor found herself responding despite herself. There was no denying, he was a good-looking guy — whoever he was. Even wearing a scruffy old pair of jeans and a red checked shirt with a black leather biker's jacket slung over the top, he was gorgeous.

His smile seemed to light up the concourse and his eyes danced with mischief as he told her funny stories about his fans. He always made sure the joke was at his own expense, not theirs, and she liked him all the better for it.

'I'm Eleanor, by the way,' she interjected at one point, holding out her hand.

'I'm . . . ' He hesitated, as though he'd been about to tell her his name and changed his mind. 'Delighted to meet you, Eleanor.' He held her hand rather than shaking it and seemed in no hurry to let go.

Eleanor tried to ignore the tingling in her fingers when their hands touched and the jolt of electricity that shot up her arm. She pulled her hand away, then regretted it. She already missed his touch. He was smiling, and she wondered if he was toying with her. Had he realised she didn't know who he was? Was he thoroughly enjoying the novelty of the situation? Or, worse still, did he assume he needed no introduction?

Eleanor bristled. She'd met too many people like that during her years in the theatre and she wasn't about to put up with it again, not even from someone as handsome as this stranger.

'Excuse me,' she said, getting up and walking over to a screen showing departures, which she could just as easily have read from where she was sitting. Yes! It looked as though the gods of air travel were smiling on her. There was her flight to Inverness and though it wasn't due to depart for a while yet, the gate number had been listed.

She went back and started gathering her belongings.

'I'd better get going, my flight should be boarding soon. It's been really nice to meet you . . . ' She hesitated, to see if he was finally going to fill in the blank by telling her his name. But he didn't and her resolve hardened. She wasn't going to fall for this handsome charmer.

He might look like the boy next door with his clean-cut good looks, but there was no doubt in Eleanor's mind that this was a dangerous man. She could feel herself starting to drown in those gorgeous blue eyes, her resistance ebbing away. Just the memory of their hands touching made her face burn. The sooner she got away the better.

'What a shame, I was really enjoying our conversation. Well, it's been lovely to meet you, Eleanor. I hope you have a good flight and a safe journey home.'

Eleanor noticed the Hollywood smile he flashed at her as he crammed on his hat and dark glasses had none of the warmth of the genuine smiles they'd shared while they sat chatting. It was as though he'd drawn a blind down, hiding his real personality and changing back into the movie star, rock star or whatever he was.

He got up and left abruptly, leaving Eleanor feeling alone and slightly bereft.

⋆ ⋆ ⋆

The flight seemed a bit tedious after her encounter with the man in the airport. Eleanor dozed for most of it, losing herself in some wonderful dreams in which her mystery man featured heavily. She woke with a start, flushed and restless. A quick glance round told her no one was looking at her, so she obviously hadn't been groaning and sighing while she slept, which was good to know. But it was disappointing to wake up and find a middle-aged snoring businessman beside her instead of the handsome hero of her dreams. She gave herself a mental shake — she had to stop thinking about him.

They'd be arriving soon and she had a hire car to collect, so she needed to be wide awake and alert to be able to drive safely. The pilot had confirmed the reason for the delays to the Scottish flights was the weather. No surprise there, but it meant she'd need her wits about her.

Eleanor rummaged in her rucksack to find her notebook. She was feeling a bit lost without her phone, which was where she'd usually keep all the information about her journey. Which hire car company had she opted for in the end? Surely she'd written down a booking confirmation number or something?

But it had all been such a rush. Eleanor had a vivid memory of jotting prices down on the back of an envelope and circling the cheapest one. Then the phone had rung just as she'd picked it up to make the booking. It was her grandmother, who had arrived home to her garbled answerphone message and wanted to know what was wrong. They'd had a long chat, during which Nana had assured her she could come and stay for as long as she wanted.

'In fact, that could work out rather well. I might ask you to do me a wee favour while you're staying with us — but we can talk about that when you're here and settled.'

That sounded ominous. Eleanor had done 'wee favours' for her nana before and had visions of herself manning a stall at the church jumble sale for hours or baking a mountain of mince pies for the village school fund raiser.

She didn't mind really, it would probably end up being fun, though chaotic, and would certainly be a change from what she had been doing.

Eleanor dragged her mind back from her telephone conversation with her grandmother and realised with a sickening certainty that after she'd hung up, she'd forgotten to phone the car hire company. That was why she had no confirmation number. She hadn't booked a car after all!

3

James was making his way out of the airport terminal when he spotted Eleanor lurking round the car hire desks. As he slowed down, he saw the woman behind the counter shake her head and Eleanor pick up her rucksack and join the queue at the next desk.

He hesitated and tried hard not to stare at her rear end as she bent down. It was difficult not to. He gave himself a mental shake — he was behaving like some kind of pervert!

It was just that after months and months in LA, it was great to see a real woman with proper curves. And oh what curves! He'd been drinking in the sight of Eleanor's shapely legs when he tripped over them earlier. The women he'd dated in Hollywood had been all skin and bone. He didn't find narrow, boyish hips at all attractive, even when combined with pneumatic breasts, which were invariably filled with silicone. Call him old-fashioned, but James preferred a real woman.

Despite the attraction, or maybe because of it, James tried to walk away. He didn't need any romantic entanglements — he'd come home for a rest.

He looked at Eleanor, standing in the queue, drooping with tiredness. He knew exactly how she felt. He was tired, so very tired. He'd done three movies back-to-back and he was exhausted — not so much from the filming but from everything that went with it.

There was all the publicity, the interviews where he had to answer the same questions over and over again and the endless, endless parties. If he never had to go to another party again in his life he'd be a happy man.

She looked so small and forlorn, standing there with her flowery green rucksack. He sighed. No. He couldn't walk away and leave her there.

James walked towards the desk,

trying not to draw any attention to himself. He politely excused himself as he made his way through to Eleanor and touched her gently on the arm. She spun round as if she'd had an electric shock.

'That's the third time you've frightened me half to death today,' she said, though she didn't look particularly unhappy about it.

'What's the problem? Have they lost your booking?' he asked, nodding towards the desk.

'Er . . . not exactly,' she admitted. Her cheeks flushed and James felt his heart beat a little faster. 'The truth is, in my hurry to get away, I completely forgot. And now it turns out there's some kind of festival on so everyone's fully booked — hotels too, by the sounds of it.'

'Ah, that's a bit of a problem then,' James said. He noticed a woman in the queue turn to look at him when he spoke. It probably wouldn't take her long to work out who he was. He reached out and Eleanor immediately put her hand into his. 'Come with me, I might be able to help. Is that all the luggage you've got?' he asked, when they were clear of the queue. Eleanor nodded. 'Well, that's good news. Follow me.' James started to lead the way out of the airport.

'So why were you in such a hurry to get away?' he asked.

'Er . . . it's a long story,' Eleanor answered evasively. 'Where are we going, by the way?'

'Outside,' he replied.

'Are you offering me a lift?' Eleanor asked as she ran to keep up with him. 'Is your car parked outside?'

'Yes to the first question and no to the second,' James replied, slowing down so she could catch up. He liked Eleanor, a lot, so he felt it was important to be scrupulously honest with her.

'But you don't even know where I'm going. It might be completely the opposite direction.'

'Scotland isn't exactly vast,' he replied, smiling down at her, 'and you wouldn't have chosen this airport unless it was the closest to your destination. So wherever you're going won't be that much out of my way. Where are you going, by the way?' he added.

'Tullymuir,' Eleanor replied.

James stopped dead. 'Tullymuir?' he asked.

'Yes, it's — ' Eleanor began.

'I know where Tullymuir is, thank you,' he said through gritted teeth.

'Really? That's amazing! I think you're the first person I've ever met who's actually heard of it.'

'What a coincidence,' he said sarcastically. 'But I'm afraid it is quite far out of my way after all. So I'll have to go back on that offer of a lift.'

'Oh, OK,' Eleanor replied. 'Thanks anyway. 'And goodbye,' she added, looking bemused.

James gave a curt nod, turned on his heel and walked away without saying another word. He was furious with himself. He couldn't believe he'd so nearly fallen for it — for her! He must be even more tired than he'd thought. He'd been completely taken in, convinced he was the one chasing her and not the other way round. How had she managed that?

Oh, she was good, really good, so much better than that other crazy woman who had stalked him in LA. She'd been way too obvious. Eleanor — if that was even her real name — had been much more convincing, right up until the moment she mentioned Tullymuir.

He didn't know how she'd found out that was where his parents lived, but he hoped she'd keep it to herself. James didn't think they'd be at all pleased if they had to move after all these years. In fact he knew they'd never move, but his dad would be furious if hordes of paparazzi and ravening fans descended on them.

That was why James no longer stayed in the lovely flat he owned in

Edinburgh. He'd had to stop using it after the success of the science fiction blockbuster he'd been in turned him into a household name. The first time he went home after that, there were droves of people camped out on the small green in front of the building, much to the other flat owners' annoyance and his extreme embarrassment.

Fuelled by anger James marched out of the airport into the rainy, misty night. He had an arrangement with one of the car hire firms. He texted his arrival time to them before he got on his flight in LA, and they made sure Bessie was waiting for him. There she was, parked in the usual spot. His heart lifted a little at the sight or her.

'At least you never let me down, girl,' he said, putting his hand lovingly onto Bessie's cold, metal bodywork.

★　★　★

Eleanor was left standing near the exit wondering what had just happened.

31

One minute her mystery man had been ready to drive her anywhere she wanted to go, the next he seemed furious and couldn't dump her fast enough.

She was still trying to puzzle it out as she carefully steered her tiny car along the twisting, turning roads. Were there no straight bits? She'd forgotten what the countryside round here was like — not that she could see much of it at the moment, even with the wipers going full tilt.

Eleanor had been lucky. A guy at one of the car hire places had taken pity on her. He'd let her borrow one of the Smart Cars the staff used to shuttle between the airport and their storage depot a few miles away. It wasn't supposed to be hired out — in fact no money had changed hands, she'd just had to promise on pain of death to get it back to him within the next couple of days.

That would never have happened down south, Eleanor reflected. Though she had to admit it probably wouldn't have happened up here either if the man hadn't known her grandfather from the stock car racing circuit. It seemed theirs was a small, close-knit community in which her grandfather was well known — or notorious.

Eleanor slowed down so she wouldn't miss her turning. She spotted the signpost she'd been looking for, which of course made no mention of Tullymuir, and turned left. Now she was on the home strait, she could relax a little. And that was when it struck her.

It was only when she mentioned Tullymuir that everything had gone wrong. Up until then, her mystery man had been more than happy to take her wherever she wanted to go. Afterwards he'd looked stunned, as though he'd been slapped in the face, and then furious. Why on earth would anyone react like that at the mention of sleepy old Tullymuir? Nothing ever happened there.

Eleanor whiled away the last few miles of her journey letting her imagination run riot. Maybe he went on holiday there and it rained every day. No — the man was Scottish for heaven's sake, he must be used to a bit of rain.

Maybe he'd had his heart broken by a woman from Tullymuir? In her mind Eleanor ran through all the women who lived nearby and couldn't come up with a single one who was likely to have shattered this man's world. They had their fair share of local beauties, but most were too young, too old or happily married.

Of course, being married might not stop someone falling for Mr Gorgeous, but if anyone succumbed to his charms, everyone would have known about it. Nothing stayed secret in Tullymuir for long; Aggie and Bridie made sure of that.

Just thinking about the two sour-faced, middle-aged sisters who ran the village shop and post office seemed to conjure them out of thin air. There they were, striding down the hill, arguing with each other as usual. Eleanor saw their heads swivel like searchlights towards the car as she drove past and even though she made a point of not looking in their direction, she knew without a shadow of a doubt that she'd been spotted.

Oh, great! She'd hoped to lie low for a couple of days while her grandparents made a fuss of her and get settled in before the onslaught began. But by tomorrow lunchtime at the latest, everyone in Tullymuir would know she was here and the nosier neighbours would find excuses to pop round. Everyone would want to know about life in London and her work as a hot-shot director. She'd better start getting her story straight now.

Eleanor drove the borrowed Smart Car onto the long driveway next to her grandparents' house and stopped just in front of her grandfather's Land Rover. Behind it she could see another car shrouded in tarpaulin.

It looked like the old orange VW

Beetle that had sat on the drive for as long as she could remember. She wondered why her grandfather had finally covered it up? Nana had probably been nagging him about it being an eyesore or maybe he'd finally decided to do something with it after all these years. It could be his latest project.

When her grandfather wasn't racing clapped-out old bangers he loved restoring them to their original condition. Eleanor had always marvelled at how he could take a heap of rusty old junk and transform it into something truly beautiful.

As a child she'd often helped him, passing him tools as he tinkered with an engine until it purred, or polishing and buffing pristine paintwork until it shone. She wondered what he was working on now?

She twitched the tarpaulin as she walked past and caught a glimpse of the familiar orange paintwork. She smiled. She gave the bonnet a friendly pat as she walked past and headed towards the welcoming glow of light coming from the kitchen window.

4

Eleanor loved waking up in her grandparents' house. Despite everything, just being there made her feel as though she was on holiday. Her parents were both actors and it had been very rare for their touring schedules to fit in with school holidays, so Eleanor had often been packed off to Nana and Grandpa's for weeks at a time.

As she lay in bed, she could hear sheep bleating on the hillside behind the house and the smell of bacon wafted up from the kitchen. But before she raced downstairs for a slap-up breakfast, there was something she had to do first. She dived out of her narrow single bed, flung the flowery curtains wide and gazed hungrily, at the view. If she lived to be a hundred she'd never tire of it.

The house was on the edge of the

village and from her bedroom window there was an uninterrupted view of the hills. The closer ones were lush and green, with little burns wandering among them and outcrops of rock where Hamish Murdoch's sheep were sheltering from the wind. In the distance were mountains with the purple bloom of heather giving way to the rusty copper of the bracken. And further away were some higher snow-capped peaks.

Eleanor flicked the latch and lifted the sash window, sticking her head out to breathe in the. clean, Highland air. She shivered as the cold hit her and closed her eyes. She'd never quite understood how it was possible, but the air here felt different — softer some-how, gentle but at the same time energising. The air in London always felt thin by comparison, as though it had been breathed in and out by hundreds of lungs before it made it into hers, which was probably the case.

Eleanor's stomach rumbled and she

decided the view could wait; it would still be there after breakfast. Right now she craved a full Scottish breakfast, complete with black pudding and fried bread. And she knew Nana wouldn't let her down.

It was one of their rituals: the three of them always had a full cooked breakfast on Eleanor's first morning to celebrate her arrival. After that there'd be cereal, porridge or toast as usual but for now it was time to indulge herself for a change.

Over breakfast Eleanor gave her grandparents a severely edited account of her directorial debut. She went into great detail about planning and rehearsals and glossed over the opening night disaster as much as possible.

Although she didn't lie outright, she made it sound as though her visit to them was a much-needed break after months and months of hard work and had nothing to do with running away.

She wasn't sure whether they believed her or not. Davy and Janet

Webster were nobody's fools. Janet's piercing dark eyes seemed to see through flimflam straight to the heart of the matter, as Eleanor knew from experience. But neither of them challenged her. They seemed to sense she was feeling fragile, so they welcomed her with open arms and encouraged her to rest and relax. She didn't mention the man at the airport at all, even though he was never very far from her mind.

★ ★ ★

The next day Eleanor returned the borrowed Smart Car to the airport. Her grandfather followed in his old Land Rover, so he could give her a lift home. While he chatted with his stock car racing buddy at the. car hire desk Eleanor couldn't help watching out for her mystery man, even though there was no way he could possibly be there.

By now he must be safely at his destination, doing whatever movie or rock stars did when they weren't working — presumably lounging by a pool sipping cocktails, surrounded by beautiful women. She'd never know. And the chances were she'd never see him again. The thought made her feel a bit sad, which was ridiculous seeing as she'd only met him for a couple of hours.

Then Eleanor's sense of humour came to the rescue. If he was lounging by a pool, it would have to be an indoor one seeing as they were in Scotland and it was late October. She chuckled to herself. Unless of course it was a hot tub . . . While Eleanor waited for her grandfather she lost herself in a happy daydream featuring her and Mr Gorgeous in a hot tub sipping glasses of champagne. Mmmm.

'Are you all right, love?' her grandfather asked. 'Only you seem to be away with the fairies.'

'Fine. Just daydreaming,' she said and quickly changed the subject.

★ ★ ★

It was several days before Eleanor's grandmother brought up the 'wee favour' she'd mentioned on the phone, by which time Eleanor had completely forgotten about it.

'So, Ella, your grandfather and I were wondering if you'd be able to help out with something while you're here, if you feel up to it?'

Eleanor was at the sink peeling potatoes.

'Of course. You know I'd do anything for you two,' Eleanor replied. 'Besides, I'm feeling loads better since I got here — I always do. I've often wondered if this place might be a little bit magic, you know.'

'I'm glad you feel that way because, as it happens, it's something to help Tullymuir rather than the two of us. But as you know we're a very close-knit community here, so anything you do to help the local area benefits us as well.'

Eleanor put the potato peeler down and turned to face her grandmother, who suddenly seemed very engrossed in stirring the big pot of mince on the stove. It wasn't like Janet to be so evasive and Eleanor started to feel a little uneasy. Just how many cakes would she have to bake?

'Go on,' she encouraged.

'Well, there's no point beating about the bush,' Janet said. 'The fact is, we need someone to help Katie Moore organise the Christmas panto.'

'Mrs Moore doesn't need any help, she could do it with her eyes shut!' Eleanor laughed despite the sinking feeling in her stomach. She couldn't believe she was being asked to get involved with the theatre when she'd just managed to escape and leave that world behind for a while. 'I'm sure she was probably running the amateur dramatics society before I was even born.'

'You're right, love. But that's the problem. Katie isn't getting any younger and her memory's not what it was. In fact, though she'd never admit it, I think it's more serious than just getting a wee bit forgetful with old age.'

Eleanor raised her eyebrows enquiringly.

'Unfortunately, I suspect the poor dear might have a touch of dementia. Nothing's been said, you understand, but it's pretty clear to everyone she's not herself these days.'

Eleanor's eyes filled with tears. 'But Mrs Moore was so, so ... ' She couldn't speak. Her heart was too full, her head bursting with memories: Mrs Moore marching up and down the village hall telling everyone where to stand, her high heels clattering on the wooden boards; Mrs Moore sitting at the piano teaching her how to control her breathing when she sang; Mrs Moore making up dance routines and capering round the stage demonstrating them; Mrs Moore sitting in the wings with a copy of the script during countless performances prompting anyone who forgot their lines. She was the one who'd encouraged Eleanor to pursue her dream of becoming an actress and taught her far more about acting than most of the teachers at drama school. In fact she wouldn't be surprised if it had been Katie Moore who'd got her mother's acting career started too.

'Exactly. But I'm afraid *was* is the operative word,' Davy added, walking into the kitchen with an oily rag in his hand.

'You see, she's taken to wandering,' Janet said ominously.

'And not just her mind,' Davy explained. 'I found her halfway down the road to Inverbruin the other week, wearing her housecoat and slippers. I had to help her home. She'd forgotten where she lives.'

'Poor Mrs Moore. Of course I'll do whatever I can to help, but I can hardly wade in and take over. She wouldn't thank me for that!' Eleanor added, remembering just how formidable the diminutive drama teacher could be.

'No, but we thought if you volunteered to take on one of the parts, you'd be able to help Katie out without her realising what you were doing,' Janet said a little sheepishly.

'She really can't manage,' Davy went on. 'And we're afraid if someone else doesn't take over it'll be the end of the Tullymuir Amateur Dramatics Society altogether.'

'Which would be a real shame,' Janet added. 'The society has done a panto every Christmas and a play every summer for as long as I can remember.'

Eleanor knew that only too well. As a child she'd sat in the audience clutching her programme, a box of Maltesers on her knee, heart thumping with anticipation as she waited for the velvet curtains to open and the shows to start.

She still remembered the joy and amazement of seeing the village hall transformed by Mikey's beautifully painted sets and her grandparents' neighbours equally transformed by Jacqui's rich, exotic costumes. The whole thing had been completely and utterly magical, so unlike the boring everyday world.

And it was her desire to be a part of that magic that encouraged Eleanor to move from her seat in the audience onto the stage. She'd taken part in her first panto at the age of seven, playing the part of second footman and getting such a laugh from her one and only line that she'd been hooked ever since.

'So, what do you think, Ella?'

Eleanor looked up and found Nana and Grandpa both looking at her anxiously.

After the disaster of her London play, organising the Tullymuir Christmas panto was the very last thing she wanted to do. But she could hardly tell them that without admitting what had really happened in London. And she knew she had no choice: there was no way she could turn her back on her old drama teacher now their roles were reversed and it was Katie needing her help. There was also no way she would let her beloved grandparents down. She took a deep breath.

'You haven't even told me what it is. Which panto are we doing this year?' she stalled, immediately wishing she'd said 'they' rather than 'we'.

'It's *Cinderella*,' Janet replied.

'Wasn't that the first one you were ever in?' Davy added.

Eleanor smiled. 'Yes, it was.' She didn't think she'd get away with being second footman this time. 'But surely there are no parts left by now? I bet Katie allocated them all ages ago,' she said hopefully. Maybe she could get away with just directing the panto and not having to act in it too.

'She did,' Davy chuckled. 'But that was before anyone knew Betty McCardle was pregnant. The poor lassie was so chuffed to get the lead role after all these years, she didn't let on.'

'I don't know how she thought she'd get away with it,' Janet added crossly. 'McCardle weans are always big. She's

49

already starting to show, and by the time Christmas comes she'll be the size of a hoose.'

Eleanor couldn't help smiling. Her grandmother, who was very particular about how her family spoke and had even sent Eleanor's mother to elocution lessons, always got very Scottish when in the throes of strong emotion.

'Poor Betty,' Eleanor said. 'She must be so disappointed.'

'That's one way of putting it,' Davy said.

'That doesn't excuse her making an exhibition of herself,' Janet said. 'Running up the high street weeping and wailing like a mad woman! And all over a silly play.'

Hearing the disapproval in her grandmother's voice, Eleanor was very glad she hadn't admitted to her own appalling behaviour, running away from London after her first-night disaster. But then a terrible realisation dawned. Grandpa had said Betty got the lead role, that could only mean . . .

'So what part was Betty going to be playing?' she asked, already dreading the answer.

'Why, Cinderella of course,' Janet replied.

'Cinderella?' Eleanor pulled out a kitchen chair and sat down heavily. 'I can't just turn up, swan in and take the best part! All the Tullymuir tabbies will be out to get me. They're probably sharpening their claws already!'

'What are you talking about? Sharpening their claws indeed,' Janet tutted. 'You need to stop being so melodramatic, dear. I'm sure everyone will just be relieved you're here to save the day.'

'Well, maybe not everyone,' Davy admitted. 'I think there were a fair few lassies who were keen to be swept off their feet by Craig Buchanan!'

'Craig? What's he got to do with it?' Eleanor asked warily.

'He's Prince Charming.'

5

Could things get any worse? Eleanor doubted it. Of course it made sense for Craig Buchanan to be playing the part of Prince Charming. No other man in Tullymuir was more suited to the role.

And she should know; she'd chosen him as her own Prince Charming many years before. He was tall and strikingly handsome, with strawberry blond hair and an impressive physique. But his muscles came from years working on the family farm rather than hours spent in the gym.

He was easy-going and good-natured, unaware of his good looks and much happier playing sports with his mates and going for a drink at The Old Thistle than charming the local girls.

For the whole of one summer, the fifteen-year-old Eleanor had hero-worshipped Craig, following him and his friends around hoping he'd notice her. Unfortunately he did . . . her hopes of romance had been dashed when he'd nicknamed her 'Jaws' after the metal-toothed villain from the James Bond movies.

The Tullymuir cinema always showed old movies since new releases were too expensive for their limited budget and that summer they'd opted for a James Bond season. It was just unfortunate for Eleanor that they coincided with her turning up at her grandparents for the summer with a fixed brace to straighten her crooked teeth.

Deep down she knew Craig had only called her Jaws to get a laugh, he hadn't meant to be cruel, but she'd still gone home and cried her heart out. She'd avoided him for the rest of her stay, spending a lot of time wandering the braes and finding places to sit and read. That was the year she read *Crime And Punishment*. The gloomy Russian tome suited her mood exactly.

Eleanor smiled to herself. She'd had

her revenge, or rather her moment of triumph, a couple of years later. She'd returned to Tullymuir without spots, bronzed from a rare holiday in France with her parents, slim and with a stunning smile courtesy of the hated brace.

Craig's reaction when he saw her had been comical. He'd done a double-take like a cartoon character, his eyes out on stalks with open admiration. He'd spent the rest of the summer pursuing her. Eleanor remembered lapping it up. She'd made him suffer for a while, of course, forced him do plenty of chasing before she let him eventually catch her. But that was followed by many happy hours of kissing and canoodling in his father's barn.

It might not sound like the most romantic place on earth, but it was warm, dry and private and they were both too young and eager to be bothered by the roughness of the straw or the occasional mooing of a cow.

Unfortunately it wasn't long before

Eleanor discovered that Craig's mind wasn't as well developed as his muscles. She was soon bored by the endless conversations he and his friends had about sports and frustrated by having to laboriously explain any joke she made. She and Craig definitely weren't on the same wavelength.

By the time she left Scotland at the end of that summer, she was glad to bring their relationship to an end. It had been fun while it lasted, but there was no future in it.

Poor Craig seemed to think differently and was heartbroken when she left. But by all accounts he soon recovered when shooting season started, so she didn't feel too badly about it. On subsequent visits to Tullymuir she didn't exactly avoid him but she did make a point of not spending too much time in his company. So she definitely didn't want to play Cinderella to his Prince Charming. If she was honest with herself, Eleanor still had a bit of a soft spot for Craig, who'd been her first love, and she was worried he might get the wrong idea.

As Eleanor walked down the High Street, which was too narrow and quiet to deserve such a grand name, she wondered how she could possibly keep Craig at arm's length while they were playing lead romantic roles opposite each other. She was still pondering this when she wandered into the shop to pick up some milk for her grandmother.

'Ah, here she is — the hot-shot director from London's West End,' a harsh voice announced.

Eleanor looked up, her face flushing as she found herself being stared at by the queue of people waiting in line at the post office counter. Bother! She should have anticipated this, but she'd been too busy thinking about Craig.

Aggie McBride's gimlet eyes held hers for a moment and sparkled maliciously. Eleanor knew from experience that she'd happily ignore the queue on the other side of the counter while she had a long, shouted conversation with someone on the other side of the shop. Though in this case, Eleanor suspected it would be more of an interrogation than a conversation.

She said hello, smiled vaguely and quickly made her way towards the chilled cabinet for some milk. Aggie's sister Isobel, who for some reason was always known as Bridie rather than by her first name, was standing at the till.

'We hear you're going to be directing our own little panto. I'm surprised the Tullymuir Dramatic Society isn't beneath your notice now you're so successful, even though we were the ones who nurtured your talent,' Bridie simpered, giving a little giggle. Somehow she managed to make the word talent sound like an insult.

And that's how they worked: angular harsh-voiced Aggie lurking like a spider behind the post office counter and her round, giggling sister Bridie wedged behind the shop till. They trapped people in a kind of pincer movement and wouldn't let them leave until they'd squeezed every last morsel of information out of them.

'News travels fast around here,' Eleanor said, giving them both a beaming smile as she picked up a carton of milk. There were times when she was very glad to have years of professional acting training behind her.

'So it's true then? You've come to take over and show us how it's meant to be done,' Aggie rasped, her forty-a-day habit coming through in her voice.

'Not really. But then, most rumours and gossip aren't all that accurate, are they? I've simply been asked to stand in for Betty McCardle. I wasn't planning on taking over unless Mrs Moore wants me to, in which case I'd be extremely flattered and delighted to help an old friend,' Eleanor concluded, hoping that would be the end of it.

She should have known better.

'Aye, it's such a shame about Katie Moore,' Bridie said, the sorrowful face she put on not quite masking the delight in her eyes. 'You'll find her very much changed since you were last here. But then it's been a few years now since you've visited us, what with you being so busy.'

'Very much changed? Away with the fairies more like!' Aggie added harshly, giving a grating laugh that turned into a hacking cough.

Eleanor was shocked. How could anyone be so cruel? Especially about a friend and neighbour who'd done so much for Tullymuir over the years. But that was Aggie for you, heartless and bitter to the bone. Eleanor saw a few people in the queue shuffling around uncomfortably but no one challenged Aggie — they didn't want her harsh gaze and wicked tongue turned on them. Eleanor could feel her anger rising, but before she could find the words to defend her old teacher, the sisters had moved on.

'You mustn't feel too bad about stealing the lead role though,' Bridie reassured her, with a false smile. 'I'm sure you're much better suited to playing Cinderella than any of our own homegrown talent.'

'I don't feel bad about it, and I didn't steal it,' Eleanor retorted through gritted teeth. She only just managed to stop herself saying it was the last thing she wanted to be doing. 'I've only agreed to take part as a favour to my grandparents. If anyone else comes forward, I'd be delighted to step aside. I came up here for a rest, not to get involved in another production.' She put the money for the milk on the counter, relieved to have the exact amount so she could pay and go.

'Heavens above!' Bridie exclaimed. 'There's no need to take on so.'

Eleanor stiffened. Her brain started working feverishly. Was that a reference to her London play? Was it a deliberate taunt, or was she just being completely paranoid?

'Though I doubt anyone would be bold enough to put themselves forward now,' Bridie continued, her eyes glittering. 'They wouldn't feel able to compete with a professional like yourself.'

'A rest, is it?' Aggie demanded. 'Well I'm sure it's well deserved after the success of your big London play.'

Eleanor could feel the colour drain from her face. The sisters had mentioned the play twice now. News of her opening night disaster must have reached Tullymuir already. Her eyes flickered towards Aggie but thankfully her grandfather's friend, Tommy, spoke up from his place in the queue.

'Congratulations, Eleanor. You've done us all proud,' he said.

There were murmurs of approval and congratulations from other people as well. Eleanor breathed a sigh of relief. They obviously didn't know the worst yet.

That gave Eleanor the courage to hold her head high as she left the shop and again her years of training came to the rescue.

'Thank you, Tommy,' she said graciously. 'I just try and do the best I can and I'll do the same for Tullymuir's presentation of *Cinderella*. If I'm given the chance,' she added, looking pointedly at Aggie and Bridie.

Then she made her escape. It hadn't been a bad exit, as exits went. But those two old cats really were poisonous. If Aggie and Bridie were so scathing now, she couldn't even imagine how much they'd gloat and rub it in when they discovered what had really happened in London.

Eleanor shuddered and the thought came to her that they'd make the perfect Ugly Sisters for the panto, though no one would be brave enough to suggest it. They wouldn't even need to act, or wear any make-up . . .

Eleanor stopped herself before any more nasty thoughts came into her mind. Goodness, if that was the effect of ten minutes in the McBride sisters' company, she'd have to give them a wide berth from now on.

The list of people she wanted to avoid was getting longer. First Craig, now Aggie and Bridie — and she'd no idea how she was going to manage it. It looked as though her plan to visit her grandparents for a rest wasn't such a good one after all.

6

Eleanor approached the village hall that night with trepidation, her head filled with gloomy thoughts.

The walk down the hill from her grandparents' house was spooky in the dark. Their metal garden gate creaked when she opened and closed it. It probably did that all the time, but during the day she didn't notice it.

Eleanor picked up her pace as she reached the churchyard wall. Her eyes were drawn to the looming mass of the church and the gravestones in front of it. The crumbling stones formed strange shapes in the darkness and seemed to be set at crazy angles as though they were moving. Eleanor, who was focused on getting past the spooky graveyard as quickly as possible didn't notice the small figure coming round the corner until she collided with it.

She shrieked with fright and felt her heart thumping as something wrapped itself around her lower legs.

'Can you no' watch where you're goin', hen?' old Mrs Higgs asked, as she tried to untangle her dog's lead from around Eleanor's ankles.

'Sorry, Mrs Higgs,' Eleanor said, a little breathlessly. When she and Alfie were untangled, Eleanor stooped to pat the tiny chocolate brown poodle at her feet. She chatted to Mrs Higgs for a few minutes, which helped calm her down, especially as the older woman seemed completely oblivious to the darkness, the shadows and their proximity to the graveyard.

By the time she walked into the village hall a few minutes later Eleanor was feeling much better. As she opened the door, she was met by warmth, light and the sound of familiar voices.

She spotted her old friend Fiona Johnstone on the other side of the hall and began to relax a little. At least she had one close ally and staunch supporter. Some of her fears about playing opposite Craig, supplanting Betty McCardle in the lead role and surreptitiously taking over the directing from Mrs Moore, began to seep away. Especially as there, in the midst of it all, was Mrs Moore herself, looking the same as always.

Maybe her grandparents had been exaggerating and Katie Moore wasn't as bad as they'd implied. At that moment she turned and beckoned to Eleanor.

'Come on in, Betty. Don't lurk at the door, dear. We're all waiting for you so we can get started.'

'Er . . . It's Eleanor, Mrs Moore, not Betty,' Eleanor said, slightly taken aback. 'Though I'm hoping to stand in for her if that's OK with you?'

'Of course it is, dear. How lovely to see you again! You mustn't mind me, I get a bit muddled with names these days.'

After a round of greetings from the rest of the cast, some of whom seemed more pleased to see her than others, Eleanor noticed Betty McCardle walking purposefully towards her. This was the moment Eleanor had been dreading.

Her grandparents had warned her Betty didn't take it well when she had to give up the lead role. Now Eleanor was stepping into her shoes, or rather glass slippers, and she had no idea how Betty was going to behave towards her.

Emotions ran high in the theatre and actors were notoriously volatile, even amateur ones. Was Betty going to make a scene, shout and swear at her, slap her face? Everyone stopped what they doing and waited with bated breath, keen to witness the moment when the two Cinderellas met.

The hall was suddenly very quiet, the only sounds those made by Mrs Moore rifling through her handbag and muttering about finding her glasses, which were perched on top of her head.

When Betty was only a few feet away,

she stopped and locked eyes with Eleanor. Her expression was hard to read, but her eyes glittered dangerously. She didn't speak for a full minute, giving the tension in the room time to build even further. Eleanor felt like a gunslinger at the OK Corral waiting for the shootout to begin; she could feel her palms starting to sweat.

Then it dawned on her what Betty was doing. She'd obviously come to terms by now with the fact that not even the Tullymuir Amateur Dramatic Society could get away with having a heavily pregnant Cinderella. But she was determined to make the most of her one and only moment in the spotlight, and who could blame her?

'You might as well have this,' Betty said, tossing her long blonde hair out of her eyes and thrusting a well-thumbed copy of the play at Eleanor. 'After all, I'm not going to be needing it any more, am I?' she added, ending with a sob.

She stepped back and made a point

of stroking her already rounded stomach. Eleanor was unsure whether this was to console herself, comfort her baby or remind everyone why she was having to step down, but it was a very effective gesture. She couldn't help thinking Betty would have made a wonderful Cinderella: the woman had excellent timing and an obvious flair for the dramatic.

'Thank you, Betty,' she said, accepting the script far more graciously than it was given. 'I really appreciate you giving me your own copy.'

As Betty obviously expected more, she flicked through the pages and added, 'I see you've made plenty of notes in the margins, that'll be really helpful at getting me up to speed.'

Betty gave her a curt nod.

'I hope you'll all bear with me,' Eleanor said, turning to address the rest of the cast. 'I don't know my lines or anything, so I'm not going be nearly as good a Cinderella as Betty has been.'

There were several sighs of relief, or

maybe people just released the breath they'd been holding in and the hall erupted with a spontaneous round of applause. Whether this was intended for Betty or Eleanor was unclear, but Betty evidently thought it was for her, as she gave a little bow. Eleanor couldn't help catching Fiona's eye, which had an appreciative gleam in it, and she had to work very hard not to giggle. Then Betty stepped forward and shook Eleanor's hand. A truce had been called. At last everyone could settle down to the serious business of rehearsing.

Craig gestured for Eleanor to sit beside him, but thankfully there was a spare chair near Fiona. The two friends gave each other a quick hug, but they only had time to exchange a few words before Mrs Moore called everyone to order.

They were doing a quick read through of Act One for Eleanor's benefit, when Fiona nudged her and gestured towards Craig who was obviously trying to catch

Eleanor's eye. From then on every time Eleanor looked up he was watching her and smiling. Once he even winked. And though she hated to admit it, he was looking particularly good. He was sprawled at his ease on one of the plastic chairs, his jeans and black T-shirt fitting like a glove and showing off his magnificent physique. Eleanor had forgotten quite how attractive Craig was and had to keep reminding herself he was a complete and utter blockhead to stop herself from smiling back at him.

Thankfully they didn't stay seated for long. Mrs Moore soon had them all up on their feet. Eleanor enjoyed just being one of the cast again, it was such a relief to be following directions instead of having to give them.

But her respite was short-lived: as the evening wore on she found herself having to step in more and more to guide and advise the others when Mrs Moore gave confusing advice.

'Right Moira, this is when you tell Cinderella she won't be going to the ball, so I want you to be mean about it, really sneer at her,' Mrs Moore said. 'What's the problem?' she added, when Moira Brewer hesitated.

'Er, Katie, I'm playing the Fairy Godmother,' Moira offered diffidently.

Seeing the blank look on Mrs Moore's face, Eleanor's eyes skimmed down the list of characters. Thankfully Betty had scribbled everyone's name next to their part.

'Of course you are, Moira,' Eleanor said. 'It's Margaret who's the Wicked Stepmother this time,' she added, hoping this would jog Mrs Moore's memory. But Katie just looked confused.

Eleanor drew Margaret Reid towards her saying, 'Katie's quite right, we want our Wicked Stepmother to get plenty of boos from the audience. So you should have a cold, supercilious look on your face, Margaret — like this,' she added, demonstrating. Not that she really needed to; the look on Margaret's face would have curdled milk. 'Maybe you could pick your skirt up to keep it out of the dirty ashes and back away from me when I step forward to plead with you to let me go to the ball.'

And with that, everything was back on track — until the next time Mrs Moore got names muddled and told Craig, who was playing Prince Charming, to help Cinders with her chores instead of Tommy, who was Buttons the Footman.

Eleanor was annoyed with Craig and the rest of the cast. She'd always struggled with her temper, blaming it on her red hair, but the truth was she found people's lack of common sense infuriating. Surely they all knew about Katie's problem? They could easily accommodate it and work round it if everyone just ignored the names Katie called people by, listened to her advice for each character — which was always sound — and only follow it if it related to them. It really wasn't rocket science!

Part of the problem seemed to be that, although Mrs Moore was forgetful and confused, she was still decisive and forceful when it came to issuing instructions. As a result, her friends and neighbours were loath to ignore her directions even when they were obviously wrong. The result was complete chaos.

Eleanor did her best, trying to make light of the situation and keep things moving, but she could see it was going to be an uphill battle.

By the time the rehearsal was over she was exhausted and just wanted to go home, have a mug of hot chocolate and get to bed. But as she helped put the chairs away and started to gather her belongings, including Betty McCardle's copy of the script so she could learn her lines, people kept coming up to her to have a quiet word. Most of them wanted to discuss their role, suggest changes to their lines or casually mention an item of costume that would be ideal for them.

Eleanor was annoyed. She'd hoped to join the cast, go along to rehearsals like everyone else and gradually take on some of Katie's responsibilities to make life easier for the poor woman. But it was obvious that everyone knew exactly what was going on and more or less expected her to take over right away.

How could word have spread so fast? Her grandmother only broached the subject with her a couple of days ago. Then she remembered her trip to the village shop that morning. Even so, Aggie and Bridie's gossip mill must have been working overtime to have reached the entire cast by the end of the day.

At least talking about the pantomime was preferable to answering questions about her London play, which everyone inevitably seemed to want to know about. Eleanor deflected as many questions as she could and made her answers as evasive as possible. She wasn't going to lie, but neither was she prepared to admit the whole ghastly truth.

She was so busy trying to field

questions and politely extricate herself from a conversation with Hamish Murdoch, who was playing one of the Ugly Sisters, that she didn't notice Craig Buchanan lying in wait for her.

'I'll walk you home,' he said as she stood at the door trying to put her coat on while juggling her script and shaking hands with someone at the same time.

'Thanks, Craig, but I was going to walk back with Fiona,' she improvised. 'As you can imagine, we've got a lot of catching up to do.'

'So have we,' Craig replied, taking her arm. 'Now have you got everything you came with?' he added in a low voice, giving Eleanor a meaningful look, which she wasn't sure how to interpret.

'I think so,' she answered hesitantly. 'Why?'

'Shh, I'll tell you in a minute,' he murmured.

Before Eleanor could respond or object, Craig had said a loud goodbye to everyone on their behalf, relieved her of the script and tucked her arm into his. He then firmly closed the door behind them and started walking her up the hill to her grandparents' house.

'I'll bet you're glad to get out of there,' he said, showing a rare flash of insight.

'Well, yes I am,' Eleanor was forced to admit.

She also hated to admit to herself that she was actually glad to have Craig beside her as she walked up the dark road past the graveyard. She didn't exactly believe in 'ghosties and ghoulies and things that go bump in the night' but it was easier not to believe in them with Craig at her side. That made her feel like a total wuss and she tried to slip her arm out of his, but he had a tight hold of her and wasn't letting go.

Although she didn't like the possessive way he was behaving, she did like the solid, reassuring feel of his muscled arm under her hand. It had been hot in the hall and she tried not to notice the familiar musky, sandalwood smell of his body. Why did he have to smell so good?

'So what was all that about, back at the hall?' she asked, trying to stay focused.

'I suppose people are just interested in what you've been getting up to in London,' Craig answered, getting the wrong end of the stick as usual. 'I'd like to know myself actually. I expect Tullymuir must seem very dull by comparison.'

Eleanor didn't dignify that with a response. Of course London was more interesting than a tiny village in the middle of nowhere, where nothing ever happened. There was no comparison.

'No, not that, I get why everyone was bombarding me with questions about London. I mean all that cloak and dagger stuff as we came out of the hall, about whether I had everything with me.'

'Oh that, well . . . ' Craig raised an eyebrow. 'Tullymuir might not be London but we do have our own excitement, you know. It's quite a mystery actually. You see, things have been going missing at rehearsals.'

'What sort of things?' Eleanor asked.

'Well, so far, Margaret's gold pen, Moira's spare glasses, Tommy's pen-knife and my phone.'

'But no purses or wallets?' Eleanor asked.

'Not yet,' Craig confirmed.

'That's a bit odd, don't you think? Thieves usually go for hard cash or at least items with some monetary value. I doubt Moira's spare glasses would sell for much!'

'A thief? Here in Tullymuir? Don't be ridiculous!' Craig retorted.

Eleanor found his firm belief that nothing bad could happen in Tullymuir quite touching, but she knew he had a point. It wasn't that the locals were so much more upright and moral than the rest of the population, just that in such a small, close-knit community you couldn't get away with anything. Sneeze once, in the privacy of your own home, and the next day everyone would be asking how your cold was.

Stealing was pretty much out of the question unless you wanted to be branded a thief for the rest of your life, or were prepared to move away when people found out. So that left two options: either someone was deliberately trying to cause trouble, or a person whose memory was failing was absent-mindedly collecting items when people left them lying.

Eleanor almost hoped it was a disgruntled member of the cast, someone who didn't get the role they wanted, rather than poor Mrs Moore. The woman had enough to deal with, without adding unintentional theft to her problems.

'When did things start to go missing?' she asked tentatively, not sure she wanted to know the answer. 'Was it right away?' When Craig looked at her blankly she prompted, 'Or was it after the parts had been allocated?'

'I don't really remember,' he said,

turning a puzzled face towards her. She could almost hear the cogs turning. 'Are you saying someone might be deliberately sabotaging the pantomime because they're not happy with the part they got?' he asked, eventually.

'Well, I've known it to happen,' she replied.

'In that case we've got quite a few suspects,' Craig said enthusiastically. 'Margaret might look like the perfect Wicked Stepmother but I know for a fact she wanted to play the Fairy Godmother, and everyone knows how furious Betty was to be dropped as Cinderella. It could easily be one of them,' he added, warming to his theme.

Eleanor decided she'd better step in quickly. She didn't want him to start sleuthing or, worse still, making wild accusations.

'Let's not get carried away, Craig. We can't go around accusing people without evidence. Besides, if it started before everyone was given their parts it can't be a disgruntled cast member.

And it's far more likely people have either misplaced items at home or accidentally picked up someone else's belongings with their own. There's probably an innocent explanation.'

Even as she spoke, Eleanor wondered whether it might be wise to check Mrs Moore's capacious handbag at the next rehearsal or even to visit her at home and have a little mooch around. That way, if Katie had been taking things, Eleanor could see they got returned to their rightful owners with as little fuss and bother as possible and end the gossip and speculation.

What with sorting out the pantomime and a bit of detective work it looked as though she was going to have her hands full. It seemed that Craig was right, life in Tullymuir wasn't as uneventful as she'd thought.

Eleanor was still mulling everything over when they arrived back at her grandparents' house. She'd almost forgotten Craig was with her. He wasn't a great talker, unless the subject was sport, and she'd been deep in thought. So it came as a complete surprise when she found herself being swept into his arms and thoroughly kissed.

For a few blissful seconds her body just responded naturally, her lips moving against Craig's, their bodies pressed together. Craig always had been a very good kisser. Then her brain kicked in and she realised she'd made a terrible mistake. She was supposed to be keeping Craig at arm's length, not encouraging him. She pulled away.

'Craig, I really don't think this is a good idea,' she said, trying to catch her breath.

'Why not?' he asked, attempting to pull her back into his arms.

'Well for starters we've got to work together on the panto for the next six weeks and it's never a good idea to get involved with someone you're working with.'

'Surely a bit of on-stage chemistry between the two leads is a good thing?' Craig argued.

'Unless of course they have a tiff or end up splitting up and hating the sight of each other.'

'But that won't happen to us, Ella, we've known each other for years.'

Craig's use of her nickname riled her. Only family and close friends got to call her Ella, and he didn't qualify as either.

'We're a really good fit for each other. I never did understand why you broke things off,' he added sadly.

'That's the other reason, Craig. When Christmas is over I'll be going back to London.'

'You don't have to, though. You could stay here in Tullymuir. We could get married.'

7

Eleanor woke up the next morning feeling uneasy. She'd had very strange dreams and hadn't slept at all well.

It took a few minutes for her sleep-clogged brain to work out what was bothering her. Then she sat bolt upright. Craig Buchanan had proposed to her last night! On her grandparents' doorstep! Completely out of the blue!

Eleanor didn't know whether to laugh or cry. She'd said 'No' of course, and had let him down gently when she realised he was serious. But what she'd really wanted to do was tell him not to be so silly and ask where on earth such an insane idea had come from in the first place.

Setting aside the fact they'd only just met again for the first time in ages, when they'd gone out that summer nearly ten years ago it had been obvious

— to her at least — that they weren't at all compatible. How could he possibly think, after a couple of hours spent in his company at a rehearsal, a ten-minute walk up the road and one kiss that she'd be willing to marry him and spend the rest of her life in Tullymuir?

Eleanor didn't know whether to be angry with him or flattered that someone actually wanted to marry her. She'd had a few boyfriends over the years, but they'd mainly been fellow actors and none of the relationships had been serious enough for marriage to be a possibility.

She had to remind herself it wasn't a serious possibility this time either; Craig had just got carried away. And, more to the point, she had no desire whatsoever to marry him. But she realised she'd have to be a lot more careful from now on.

It had been wrong to let him kiss her last night. It had given the poor guy completely the wrong idea and she definitely wouldn't let it happen again.

But, in her defence, she'd been very tired after the rehearsal and upset too. She'd tried not to let it show, but seeing Mrs Moore so changed had been a real shock.

'So how did it go last night?' her grandmother asked at breakfast.

Eleanor dropped her knife on her plate, knocking the toast off onto the table.

'What? Oh, you mean the rehearsal.'

'What else would I mean?' Janet asked suspiciously.

'Oh, nothing,' Eleanor replied. Her head was so full of Craig's proposal, the state of Mrs Moore's mental health and the possibility of a thief in the cast that she hadn't been sure which her grandmother was asking about. She really hoped Nana and Grandpa hadn't seen her and Craig kissing on their doorstep.

'You seem a bit jumpy, Ella,' her grandfather observed. 'Are you all right?'

'I'm fine, just fine. The rehearsal was pretty full-on, though. I had a bit of a showdown with Betty McCardle right at the start. Then things settled down. But you were right about Katie Moore, she's in a bad way. She can't remember anyone's name and because in a play everyone has two — their own and their character's — it's just too much for her to cope with.'

'Now you see why we asked for your help,' Janet said.

'Yes, yes, I do,' Eleanor said, nodding slowly.

'But you must say if it's too much for you,' Davy added.

Eleanor reached across the table and patted his hand in what she hoped was a reassuring way. 'I'll give it my best shot, Grandpa.'

'Good girl.' He gave her hand a little squeeze.

'No one can ask any more than that,' Janet replied, pouring more tea into Eleanor's cup.

Eleanor decided it would be best not to mention what had happened with Craig or the fact that people's belongings were going missing. She didn't want to worry her grandparents any more than they already were. Though she suspected it wouldn't be long before they found out about both on the Tullymuir grapevine.

She might not want to distress them, but she did need to talk to somebody about it all. While she was washing up the breakfast dishes and helping her grandparents with a few chores, she considered ringing Susie back in London. But it would be difficult to explain the situation up here to someone who lived so far away, both in terms of distance and life experience. What she really needed was a person who understood the intricate workings of life in Tullymuir.

'I think I might just pop round and see if Fiona's in,' she said.

* * *

Over the years, whenever Eleanor had stayed with her grandparents, she and Fiona had been thick as thieves. She remembered the two of them playing hide and seek round the village when they were children, then fancying themselves as detectives like Nancy Drew when they were a little older, and spending hours discussing boys and memorising pop songs when they were teenagers. But what she remembered most was how much they had always laughed together.

Eleanor could really do with a laugh right now and she was looking forward to a heart to heart with her old friend. It never seemed to matter how long it was between her visits, they always picked up their conversation from where they'd left off, as though they'd only seen each the day before.

She would tell Fiona everything, all about the fiasco of the play in London and even Craig's proposal. She'd ask for her advice about the thefts and her help with Mrs Moore. Eleanor's heart felt lighter as she walked out of the village towards Fiona's cottage, which was built on a corner of her parent's land.

Unfortunately she'd forgotten that the madcap friend of her childhood was now a very responsible person with a serious, grown-up job. Fiona worked long hours as a nurse at the local hospital. So Eleanor was disappointed but not particularly surprised to find her friend's car missing from the drive and no answer when she knocked on the front door. As she waited for a few minutes, hoping in vain that Fiona was in and just taking her time getting to the door, a car-pulled up. It was Mrs Johnstone, Fiona's mother.

'Hello Eleanor,' she called, opening the car window. 'It's lovely to see you. You're out of luck, though. Fiona's shift doesn't end 'til six tonight. She won't be home much before seven.'

'Oh,' Eleanor replied, disappointed.

'You could come back,' Mrs Johnstone suggested.

'I don't expect Fiona will want a

visitor after a long day at work,' Eleanor said.

'Well, if the visitor had fish and chips with them she just might!'

'Thanks, Mrs Johnstone — that's a brilliant idea,' Eleanor said, brightening up. She decided there and then to go one better and bring a bottle of wine as well as the food, even though it would mean another visit to the dreaded corner shop.

'You're welcome. It's just nice to have you back again,' Mrs Johnstone said, beaming. 'And I hear you might be staying for good this time?'

'What?' Eleanor asked, puzzled.

'Someone told me you and Craig were getting on rather well last night, that congratulations might be in order some time soon?'

Eleanor felt her mouth opening and closing like a fish.

'Ah,' Mrs Johnstone went on, 'I've obviously got the wrong end of the stick. I should know better than to listen to corner shop gossip. Sorry!'

Mrs Johnstone said goodbye and quickly drove away. Eleanor gave a scream of sheer frustration. Now she could cheerfully strangle the McBride sisters.

* * *

Fiona came to the front door wearing a fluffy blue dressing gown and a frown, a towel wrapped around her head. But Mrs Johnstone had been right, she was delighted to receive a visitor who arrived bearing a fish supper and red wine.

'Oooh, are those for me? Come in,' she said, flinging the door wide. 'You're an angel, Ella!'

'You're sure you don't mind me turning up like this?' Eleanor asked, seeing the tiredness etched on her friend's face.

'You must be joking!' Fiona replied, roughly towelling her hair dry and hanging the wet towel on the radiator. 'I was just wondering what I could be bothered to make for my tea and this beats scrambled eggs on toast any day. Let me just grab some plates and glasses.'

'Forget the plates,' Eleanor said. 'Let's just eat out of the paper. They taste better that way anyway and it'll save on the washing up.'

'You're a woman after my own heart,' Fiona said, giving her friend a grateful hug.

It was a while before they spoke again. Fiona was obviously ravenous. She'd wolfed through half her fish supper and drained a large glass of wine before she was able to slow down and chat.

'That's better,' she sighed, sitting back into a corner of the sofa. 'Just what I needed. Now, tell me what's on your mind.'

'Not until you tell me how you are. You look exhausted and half-starved. Did you have a terrible day? Was there no time for lunch?'

She encountered a pitying look from her friend.

'It was pretty much the same as usual, to be honest. We're always short-staffed, there's never enough of us to go round, so we're on our feet all day. Breaks, when we get them, don't last long. So I always kind of fallollop when I get home. Don't worry about me. That's more than enough about my day. Tell me what this is all about.'

Eleanor's own problems seemed trivial by comparison. 'Are you sure you want to know? It all seems a bit silly and unimportant now.'

'Nonsense,' Fiona said briskly, 'listening to you is better than watching *Corrie*. Your life is always so exciting and colourful. I'm dying to know what you've been getting up to. So come on, spill the beans.' She topped up their glasses, curled her feet under her and leaned forward attentively.

Eleanor wasn't sure she liked having her life compared to a soap opera, but she could see Fiona was genuinely interested and needed the distraction after the tough day she'd had. So

Eleanor set out to entertain her.

When she started to talk about her life in the theatre, she began to realise how lucky she was to have such an interesting and unusual job. OK, so it wasn't always sunshine and laughter. It was sometimes infuriating, since directing actors could be like herding cats; it was often chaotic because there was never enough time or money; but it was never boring. Every day was different. She got to work with some amazingly talented people and used her creativity to put on shows that entertained people and made them happy.

So when she described the first night disaster, warts and all, she could start to see the funny side of having a major Hollywood actor fall off the stage. And laughing about it with Fiona helped a lot. Eleanor suddenly realised that even if the reviews were appalling, it really wasn't the end of the world, no one was going to die. Knowing that Fiona's job really was a matter of life and death put things sharply into perspective.

By the end of the evening, Fiona looked sleepy but much happier. She'd even managed to stay awake long enough to give her friend some sensible advice about Craig and helpful suggestions for dealing with Mrs Moore.

Eleanor was sorry when the evening ended — far earlier than she'd expected. But when Fiona started to fall asleep she made her friend a mug of peppermint and nettle tea to take up to bed with her and headed home.

Eleanor's head was so full of ideas for the pantomime that she didn't even mind walking home in the dark. Tucked up in bed at her grandparents' house, she sipped a mug of tea and started to learn her lines.

8

Eleanor took Fiona's advice and asked the cast to arrive fifteen minutes early for the next rehearsal. She wanted to give them a pep talk before Mrs Moore arrived.

'Thank you all for making the effort to get here earlier than usual. I know it probably wasn't easy for those of you who've been at work all day or have families to cook dinner for, so don't worry, this is a one-off. I just thought it was important to clear the air.' Eleanor paused and took a deep breath. 'Look, we all know Mrs Moore is a bit forgetful these days.'

'A bit?' came a sarcastic voice from the back.

'OK, a lot,' Eleanor amended. 'But that doesn't mean she hasn't got a great deal of valuable experience and expertise to share with us. Katie Moore has been running TADS for years, organising all our plays and pantomimes, so she really knows what she's talking about. And she still gives great advice and direction, even when she's muddling our names up.'

'It's just that it makes it so hard to follow what's going on,' Moira pointed out quietly.

'I know, Moira, I understand that. But Katie can't help getting confused. So what we need to do is make things as easy for her as we can.'

Moira nodded. 'How?' she asked.

'By ignoring the fact she calls us by the wrong names,' Eleanor said, as patiently as she could.

'I see,' Moira said, frowning.

'Look, we all know what part we're playing, don't we?'

There were nods and murmurs of agreement.

'So if Mrs Moore gives direction relating to your part, just do as she says and ignore the fact she's got your name wrong. And, by the same token, if she calls your name but the advice relates to someone else's character, just ignore it and let them do it instead. It's as simple as that.'

'That's not simple at all,' Margaret piped up, 'in fact it's awfully confusing.'

'I'm not sure I follow you either, Ella,' Craig said, a frown creasing his brow.

Eleanor made a point of meeting his eye. She'd known things would be bit awkward between them tonight. It was the first time they'd seen each other since he proposed. But she was grateful to him for turning up. The last thing she needed was to find herself without a Prince Charming.

She took a deep breath. 'We need to ignore all names and only follow advice that relates to our character,' she said, making it as clear as possible.

'It would be a lot easier if you just took over,' someone said.

The words hung in the air. Everyone looked at Eleanor expectantly.

'I'll help as much as I can — that's

why I'm here. But I won't push Katie out,' Eleanor said firmly. 'She's losing her memory, I won't take this away from her as well,' she added quietly.

That was when Eleanor looked up and saw to her horror that Mrs Moore was standing in the doorway, listening. She felt herself go cold. How much had her old teacher heard? And how much of what she'd heard had she understood? The answer came all too soon.

'Thank you for your support, Eleanor dear.' Mrs Moore's voice rang out loud and clear across the quiet hall and everyone turned to look at her. 'But I can still recognise a vote of no confidence when I hear one. That being the case, I think it's time I hung up my directing hat, don't you?' And without waiting for an answer she turned and left.

Eleanor stood, rooted to the spot, too shocked by what had happened to go after her. Then her body seemed to wake up and she made a dash for the door, shouting, 'Mrs Moore — Katie — please wait!'

But Fiona stopped her.

'I think it would be better to leave it for now,' she said, gently laying a hand on Eleanor's arm. 'You don't want to upset her even more. If she's left to her own devices she might even forget all about it. Why don't you wait and go round and see her tomorrow?'

Reluctantly Eleanor decided to be guided by her friend's advice. Fiona knew a lot more about dealing with people who had mental health issues than she did. But she still felt awful and so, by the looks of it, did everyone else.

Well, nearly everyone. Margaret, looking her usual haughty self, asked, 'Well — are we going to get started or not?'

Everyone gathered themselves together and made an attempt to rehearse Act Two, but it wasn't a great success. Only Eleanor, who had worked as a professional actress for years, was able to put aside what had happened and carry on. She knew it didn't matter how she was feeling, she still had a job to do.

It wasn't easy to be lively and vivacious if you were feeling tired or sad or worried, but if that was what the role called for, that was what you did. It was what being an actor was all about.

The others didn't have years of experience to call on, and their performances were stilted and lacklustre. People forgot their lines, missed their cues and generally made a complete hash of it. Everyone was relieved when it was over and left as quickly as possible.

Fiona stayed to help Eleanor lock up.

'I hoped, at first, that Mrs Moore might not realise what was going on. But she really seemed completely with it today, she wasn't vague and woolly at all,' Eleanor remarked.

'That's the problem with dementia. There are moments of total lucidity in amongst all the muddle and confusion,' Fiona explained.

'I wonder what she'll be like when I go and see her tomorrow?' Eleanor pondered.

'You'll just have to wait and see,' Fiona said, looking sympathetic. 'I'd offer to come with you, but I'm working all day. But if I were you I wouldn't mention what happened today, unless she does. Maybe ask her advice about something in the script. Don't make a big deal of it.'

* * *

Eleanor didn't sleep well. After hours of clock watching, she got up early and made a batch of fruit scones. By the time her grandparents came down for breakfast, the golden-brown scones were sitting on a wire rack cooling. She felt jumpy all morning and was relieved when the hands of the clock eventually crept round to ten forty-five.

Surely that was a perfectly respectable time to visit an elderly lady who might like to have a lie in of a morning?

She wasn't sure, but reasoned that anyone who turned up in time for elevenses with a tin of freshly baked scones was likely to be welcome.

Even so, Eleanor hesitated outside the familiar back door before knocking. Everyone knew Katie's front door was for strangers, friends always went round to the back. But after last night she wasn't sure she qualified as a friend any more.

It took a while for Mrs Moore to answer the door, but when she did, Eleanor was relieved to find herself greeted with a smile. Her old teacher was wearing an unusual combination of clothes: a long burgundy corduroy skirt, what looked like a man's pin-striped shirt, a bobbly cardigan and flip-flops. But as Mrs Moore had always dressed outlandishly, it was impossible to tell whether her strange outfit was a reflection of her current mental state or not. Over the years Eleanor had seen her turn up to rehearsals in everything from an old pair of pyjamas to an evening gown.

'Good morning, Eleanor dear, come in.'

Eleanor stepped into the cosy, cluttered kitchen and was relieved to find it looking pretty much the same as it always had. If she was honest she'd been half expecting the place to be in a complete state. She'd been dreading going in and finding her old teacher living in squalor, unable to look after herself any more. But as Eleanor casually glanced round she was surprised to find that, if anything, the kitchen looked cleaner and tidier than usual. This was explained a few moments later when a young woman appeared carrying a bucket of cleaning equipment, which she put into the cupboard under the sink.

'All done,' she said.

'Thank you, Maggie,' Mrs Moore replied, taking a pile of notes from her purse.

The woman took the money, counted it and shook her head. 'Too much,' she said, giving several notes back. 'Remember. We agree. Twenty only.' She spoke in a strong Eastern European accent with a slight Highland lilt.

'Oh that's right, dear, I'd forgotten.'

'No matter,' she said, shrugging. She patted Mrs Moore's hand and smiled. Eleanor almost gasped. The smile had transformed the woman's face completely and Eleanor noticed for the first time quite how beautiful she was.

'I've brought scones, if you have time for a cup of tea before you go,' Eleanor said.

The woman seemed surprised to be asked, but delighted. She looked at her watch, nodded, then said she'd put the kettle on.

'You sit, we bring,' she added, guiding Mrs Moore through to the front room. Eleanor was glad to know Mrs Moore had a cleaner coming in, someone who appeared to do a lot more than just the vaccuuming and dusting. She could hear the rise and fall of voices in the sitting room as Maggie settled the old lady in her comfy armchair by the fire. It looked as though she might do quite a bit of looking after as well as the actual cleaning she was paid to do. Eleanor was just wondering whether Maggie was actually the woman's name, when she came back into the kitchen.

'My name is Natalia,' she said slowly and carefully, touching her hand to chest to emphasise the point.

'Ah yes, Mrs Moore has trouble with names these days. I'm Eleanor,' she said, smiling and holding out her hand.

Natalia nodded in understanding as they shook hands. 'My grandmother also,' she said.

So that explained why she was so good with Katie and why she took the time to do a little extra. While Eleanor went in search of plates, knives, butter and jam, she chatted to Natalia, who was setting a tray with china tea cups and saucers, spoons, a sugar bowl and milk jug. When they'd gathered everything together, Natalia looked at Eleanor appraisingly.

Then she nodded her head decisively and said, 'Maybe she also collects?'

'Collects?' Eleanor asked, not sure what Natalia meant.

'Wait, I get,' she said and opened the door leading into the pantry. She picked something up off the floor from where it had been hidden under the lowest shelf, then came back and handed a shoebox to Eleanor.

'Maybe these belong to others,' Natalia said. 'I find under chairs, rugs, strange places.'

Eleanor opened the box to find an odd collection of items. It wasn't until she spotted a gold pen that something clicked. Craig said Margaret's pen had gone missing. What else did he say had been lost? His phone. She rummaged in the box and there at the bottom was a phone. There were several pairs of glasses too, so Moira's was probably amongst those, and a old red Swiss

109

Army knife — presumably Tommy's.

'Bless you,' Eleanor said, giving Natalia a quick hug. 'I'll make sure these get back to their rightful owners.'

'Good.' Natalia looked relieved. 'Now tea.'

Eleanor left the shoebox in the kitchen. She'd pick it up on her way out. They carried the tea things into the sitting room together and found Mrs Moore having a doze. She woke up when she heard the rattle of crockery and Natalia stirring sugar into her tea.

The three women sat and chatted. Eleanor found it easier having a third person there to defuse what could have been a tricky situation. Besides, Natalia was good company. She told them a little about her family and home in Croatia in response to Eleanor's questions and listened enthralled when they were discussing the pantomime.

'I love theatre, go often at home,' Natalia said, when the other two women paused to munch their scones.

'But not here, not yet,' she added, a little sadly.

'Well we're working on a pantomime at the moment, not a play. But you're welcome to come and join us,' Eleanor offered. She went on to explain what a pantomime was and how TADS also did a play every summer.

'My English not so good yet,' Natalia said apologetically, shrugging her shoulders.

'It would soon improve if you were to join us,' Eleanor pointed out persuasively.

Natalia nodded and smiled. She seemed pleased to be asked.

'I come, but not speak. One day maybe. Now I paint, make tea, help.'

'We'd be very grateful for whatever help you can give us,' Eleanor assured her, telling her the time of the next rehearsal. She was delighted to have the hard-working, capable woman on board. She was sure Natalia would be an asset to their group.

Natalia, who'd kept glancing at the

clock, got to her feet. 'Must go. Next job,' she said, tapping her watch.

'See you on Friday then,' Eleanor said.

'Yes,' Natalia said, stooping to give Katie a kiss on the cheek as she left.

Eleanor was very relieved she'd taken Fiona's advice. It was obvious that Mrs Moore had no recollection of the previous night's events. She chatted away happily about her thoughts and plans for the panto as well as making helpful suggestions for how Eleanor should play her role. Which meant Eleanor was able to run some of her own ideas past her old friend.

'I was wondering what you thought about us adding a few lines here and there just to make it more topical, like they do in the big London pantos?' Eleanor said.

'What did you have in mind, dear?' Katie asked. 'I'm all for it, you understand, but some of the older people round here might not like it if we alter it too much.'

Eleanor had to hide a smile. It was nice to know that Katie, who must be in her late seventies at least, didn't consider herself to be old.

'Just a few throwaway lines,' she explained. 'Like the royal wedding. Maybe we, could have Cinders saying to Buttons how the chances of Prince Charming marrying her were about as slim as him marrying an American actress.'

'Brilliant,' said Katie, clapping her hands. 'I love it. But then Buttons should say something like, 'Well, it happened to Meghan, why not you?' just to make sure everyone gets the joke.'

'What about a few jokes about Donald Trump?' Eleanor asked, jotting down the line Katie had suggested.

'I don't think so,' Katie said, shaking her head. 'It's a mistake to make jokes about politics or religion, you always end up offending someone.'

It was great to have the old Katie back, even if only for a short while. It made Eleanor even more determined to keep her fully involved in the pantomime. They'd just have to work round her memory lapses and that was all there was to it!

9

The next few rehearsals went so well that Eleanor started to feel quite hopeful. She returned everyone's belongings without any fuss, saying she'd found the shoebox and its contents in the store cupboard.

Everyone pretended to believe her, whether they really did or not, with the exception of Margaret. She raised an eyebrow, looked pointedly at Mrs Moore and muttered something about leaving valuable items at home from now on.

Natalia had started coming along and was making herself invaluable. She did everything from making cups of tea to helping Jacqui sew costumes, all the while keeping a weather eye on Mrs Moore. Everyone was making a real effort: lines were learned, Mrs Moore's instructions were followed by the appropriate people, even scenery and costumes started to materialise.

The only fly in the ointment was Craig. He didn't seem to have taken Eleanor's refusal seriously. Like many not-too-bright people, once he'd got an idea in his head there was no shifting it. Every time they met around the village — and they seemed to bump into each other rather a lot — he made sly references to suitable dates and venues. He literally wouldn't take no for an answer.

When yet another person offered her their congratulations, Eleanor felt it was time to put a stop to this once and for all. She borrowed her grandfather's car and drove to the Buchanans' farm where she found Craig in the farmyard helping his father and brothers unload heavy sacks from the back of a trailer.

She ignored their smirks and knowing looks and took Craig to one side.

'You need to stop going around telling people we're getting married,' she hissed, trying to keep her voice down so Craig's brothers, who were blatantly ear-wigging, wouldn't hear. 'Mrs Higgs just stopped me and asked when the engagement party will be and what we'd like for a present.'

Craig choked back a laugh.

'It's not funny!' Eleanor retorted. 'Mrs Higgs needs her pension to live on, she can't afford to go around buying engagement presents for people who aren't even engaged.'

'I know that. And I haven't been telling anyone anything, honestly,' he added. 'You know what Tullymuir's like, news travels fast around here.'

'But this isn't news, Craig, it's nonsense — just rumours and lies. We're not getting married, not now, not ever!'

Without intending to, Eleanor had raised her voice at the end. She could feel herself being glared at even before she glanced up and saw four pairs of angry eyes watching her. Craig's father spat on the ground and one of his brothers muttered something about

117

people thinking they were too good to join the Buchanan clan.

Eleanor decided it was time to leave.

'I'm sorry, Craig,' she said. 'I didn't mean it to come out like that. But we can't let people go around thinking we're getting married when we're not. It isn't fair — on anyone.'

She walked back to her car and drove away. In the rear-view mirror she could see Craig standing in the middle of the path looking miserable and lost. For a big, muscular man he had the uncanny ability of being able to look like a small puppy — one that she'd just kicked. She wished she hadn't been quite so brutal about it. But when Craig had laughed it had made her angry, and her words had come out more forcefully than she'd intended.

She hadn't wanted to hurt him. She'd tried doing it the softly, softly way — for several weeks now. But that just hadn't got through. Eleanor sighed. Maybe this was better in the long run.

When her grandmother came back from the corner shop the next day with the news that Craig had been involved in a shooting accident, Eleanor felt sick.

'What happened?' she asked, gripping the edge of the kitchen table for support as her grandmother unpacked her shopping.

'What's the matter, Ella?' Janet asked. 'You'd better sit down. You've gone as white as a sheet.'

Eleanor sat down heavily on a kitchen chair and put her head between her knees as instructed. She heard something being put down on the table beside her and looked up to find a glass of water there. She sat up slowly and took a grateful gulp of it. The chilliness revived her a little.

'I'm not going to faint. It was just a shock, that's all. Now please tell me what's happened to Craig.'

'To be honest, I don't really know. There are rumours flying about right,

119

left and centre but no one seems to know the truth of the matter. All that's known for sure is that Craig and his brothers went out shooting yesterday afternoon and the poor lad's ended up in hospital. But whether it's serious or not I have no idea.'

'Hospital?' Eleanor asked weakly. 'No one goes to hospital unless it's serious. Oh, Nana. What have I done?'

'What do you mean?' Janet asked, giving her a piercing look. 'How can Craig's accident possibly have anything to do with you?'

'Eleanor?' she prompted, when here was no reply. 'What's this all about? Are you and Craig engaged like everyone's saying?'

'No!' Eleanor cried, bursting into tears.

'There, there, love,' Janet said, stroking Eleanor's back as she put her head in her hands and sobbed. 'Tell Nana all about it.'

Eleanor looked up, not quite able to meet her grandmother's eyes. 'I went to see Craig at the farm yesterday and told him I wouldn't marry him. Now he's gone and shot himself. It's all my fault!'

'I see. Well, for starters we don't know whether there was any shooting involved at all,' Janet pointed out calmly.

Eleanor could hear her grandmother moving about as she spoke. There was the sound of the kettle being filled and the rattle of crockery.

'Just because he had an accident when he was out shooting, doesn't mean he's got a bullet in him. If they were after rabbits, he could just as soon have cut himself with a knife skinning one of the poor creatures.'

Janet's voice was soothing and her sensible, no-nonsense attitude began to filter through to Eleanor. Maybe she was jumping to conclusions.

'And if he has been shot, there's nothing to say he did it himself. It's just as likely one of those big galumphing brothers of his missed their target and winged him instead.'

The kettle boiled. Eleanor smelled the mug of hot, steaming tea her grandmother put on the table beside her. She lifted her head, dried her eyes and took a sip. It was sweet and comforting.

'That's better, love. Now just calm down a little and see sense,' Janet said. 'You've always had an over-active imagination.'

Eleanor started to protest.

'No, I'm not scolding you. I know it's your imagination that makes you such a good actress. That, and being able to put yourself in other people's shoes. But it does mean you can get a bit carried away at times and you take things too much to heart. Now why don't you tell me all about it? What exactly has been going on?'

Eleanor took a deep breath and launched into her tale. She felt much better when she'd told her grandmother everything. For starters, it made her realise there wasn't that much to tell.

Craig had proposed, she'd refused. That should have been the end of it. It was the rumours and gossip that had caused everything to spiral out of control. That, and Craig refusing to take no for an answer.

'Well, I can't see that you've done anything you need to be ashamed of,' Janet concluded, when she'd listened to the end without interrupting.

'I probably shouldn't have let Craig kiss me that night after the first rehearsal,' Eleanor admitted.

'Maybe not,' her grandmother agreed, smiling unexpectedly. 'But Craig Buchanan is a handsome man and it's easy to get carried away when you're young. We've all done it.'

'Even you, Nana?' Eleanor asked, not quite able to imagine her stern grandmother getting carried away with anything.

'Yes, Eleanor, even me,' she replied. 'But you can close that open mouth of yours because I'm not about to tell you anything.'

'Oh. So what do you think I should do?'

'There's nothing much you can do, at least until we find out exactly what's happened.'

'I could phone the hospital?'

'I doubt they'd give out any information as you're not a relative. You'll just have to wait.'

Patience wasn't Eleanor's strong point.

'I could drive to the hospital — or even out to the Buchanan's farm,' she offered.

Janet raised her eyebrows. 'I really don't think that's a good idea, do you?'

'No. I suppose not. I don't expect his family would be pleased to see me at the moment.'

'Exactly,' Janet agreed. 'So you'll just have to wait, with as much patience as you can muster. Now, how about you help me bake a cake for my SWI meeting tomorrow night?'

Ah, cake making. Eleanor had been wondering how long it would be before she got roped into doing that! But of course her nana was right as always: concentrating on measuring out the butter, sugar and dried fruit, setting them on the hob with some water to simmer, kept her hands busy and her mind occupied.

'So this is why your fruit cakes are so moist!' Eleanor said. 'You soak the dried fruit first.'

'That's right. But it's a trade secret — so don't you go telling everyone.' Janet pretended to admonish her.

'I won't,' Eleanor promised, grinning.

Having something to do was helping a lot. By the time the flour, mincemeat — 'oooh, a secret ingredient!' — and egg had been added to the cooled mixture, Eleanor was feeling a lot better. But when the cake was in the oven and she'd done the washing up and wiped down the surfaces, Eleanor started to get agitated again. Thankfully, just as she'd made another round of tea for herself and her grandparents and was sitting down, her hand curled round the handle and a glum look on her face, Fiona turned up.

'Mmmm, lovely smell, Mrs W,' she said, coming in to the kitchen through the back door. Then she seemed to register the solemn faces round the table. 'Who's died?' she asked.

'Don't say that! Don't even think it!' Eleanor gasped, looking ghostly pale.

'We're very much hoping Craig Buchanan hasn't,' Janet said.

'Craig? Are you serious?' Fiona said, obviously trying hard not to laugh. 'Why would he have died? He's only broken his ankle.'

'His ankle?' Eleanor repeated.

'Yes. He tripped over one of the dogs when he was out shooting yesterday and ended up with his foot down a rabbit hole. He's broken his ankle, that's all.'

'Oh, what a relief! So I didn't kill him after all!'

Fiona looked puzzled, so Eleanor had to explain what had been going on all over again. Now she knew the truth,

Eleanor was able to laugh about it all — both at herself for getting so worked up over nothing and at Craig's ridiculous accident.

'Everyone's going to tease him unmercifully when he comes to the TADS rehearsal tomorrow night,' she finished.

'Ah,' Fiona said. 'About that. Depending on how bad the break is, Craig will have a cast on his foot and be hobbling around on crutches for anywhere between six and twelve weeks.'

'Poor Craig,' Eleanor said. 'That's going to make it difficult for him to help around the farm.'

'Er, it's also going to make it impossible for him to be in the panto,' Fiona pointed out. 'I think you're going to have to find yourself another Prince Charming.'

10

Finding a new Prince Charming wasn't going to be easy. The problem nearly drove Eleanor to drink . . . or rather, it drove her and Fiona to The Old Thistle that evening to discuss the situation over a few glasses of wine.

Even though it might be difficult to find a suitable replacement for Craig, Eleanor wasn't feeling too down-hearted. The immense relief of knowing she wasn't responsible for his accident had put her in such a buoyant mood that nothing was getting to her. She walked down the road arm in arm with her friend, enjoying the views of the hills in the distance and laughing over the sillier suggestions Fiona made for Craig's replacement.

'He must be seventy-five if he's a day!' Eleanor objected to the latest candidate, giggling.

As it turned out, The Old Thistle was the best place to go. There was a football match on the television and the bar was filled with men. The atmosphere crackled with testosterone, good natured banter and just a hint of underlying danger. Just about every man from the village and the nearby homes and farms was there, holding a pint, eyes glued to the screen.

As the two women sat in a cosy corner near the fire, surreptitiously examining the men gathered round the flat-screen television in the bar, Eleanor was reminded of their conversations when they were teenagers. This time it was a lot trickier though, as it wasn't just a case of who they fancied. Suitable candidates not only had to be reasonably good-looking, they had to be well-spoken and open to the idea of taking part in the local panto. So they either needed someone with hidden acting talents just waiting to be discovered, or a man with a good sense of humour who'd at least be willing to give it a go.

Once she'd stopped suggesting the most unsuitable males in the whole of Tullymuir — from Bob Roberts with his flat cap to little Johnny Mirelli who was all of six years old — Fiona's help was invaluable. When Eleanor dredged up the name of some handsome lad she remembered from summers at her grandparents, Fiona was able to tell her what had happened to the boy in question.

'Got a job down in Glasgow,' she replied in answer to one of Eleanor's queries. 'Married an American girl and moved to San Francisco,' she said to another. 'Have you seen what he looks like these days?' she asked about a third, puffing her cheeks out and drawing an invisible beer belly with her hand. And as Fiona's local knowledge was far more up to date than Eleanor's, she was able to suggest a few possibles Eleanor didn't even know about.

'What about him?' Fiona asked,

nodding towards Adam, the handsome Aussie barman.

'He's quite a looker, but unless he can tone down that accent I think the audience might struggle to understand what he's saying.'

'Hugh Jackman's Australian,' Fiona said.

'Yes, but he's also a professional actor with access to the best voice coaches in the world,' Eleanor retorted.

They both looked up when there was an explosion of laughter from the bar.

'You could've told me you wanted it for the football table, mate! What am I supposed to do with this?' Adam asked in his cheerful Antipodean tones, holding up what looked like a glass of orange juice with a straw in it.

'See what I mean?' Eleanor asked. 'Looks like a breakdown in communication — *Balamory* meets *Home And Away*.'

'The lads are just taking the mickey,' Fiona explained. 'I bet they asked him for a screwdriver to fix the football table knowing he'd mix them a vodka and orange.'

They sat and sipped their drinks in silence for a few minutes, racking their brains and trying not to be distracted by the immaculately groomed football player who'd just scored a goal.

'Ooooh, I know!' Fiona said, the wine making her less coherent but more enthusiastic.

'Yep, he'd be perfect,' Eleanor commented. 'Look at his hair. All that running around and not a single strand out of place — now that takes some doing! But I doubt he's available to do panto, though you never know these days.'

'Would you shut up about that football player for a minute? I've just thought of someone who'd be perfect. What about Andrew McFarlaine?'

'Who's he?' Eleanor asked, dragging her eyes reluctantly from the screen. 'I don't think I remember an Andrew McFarlaine.'

'You wouldn't,' Fiona said. 'He

132

joined the local practice out at Inver-bruin recently when old Dr Willis finally retired.'

Eleanor noticed her friend's flushed cheeks and demanded to be told more. Apparently Dr McFarlaine was young, good-looking and unattached.

Eleanor's mind started to race. If they could convince him to play Prince Charming, maybe Fiona could replace her as Cinderella? It would be much easier for Eleanor to direct the pantomime if she had a bit part. And that way Fiona could fall in love with Dr McFarlaine as Prince Charming — if she hadn't already.

Eleanor could smell romance in the air. She was keen to help her friend find the man of her dreams. The poor girl worked far too hard and didn't have nearly enough fun for someone their age.

The two women drifted through the rest of the evening, floating on romantic daydreams and wine, but not coming to any conclusions about a suitable replacement for Craig. Even though Eleanor hated to admit it, he was going to be a hard act to follow: he certainly looked like a handsome hero even if he didn't always behave like one.

Her mind kept wandering back to the man at the airport. Now he would be perfect! She remembered his gorgeous smile, how the corners of his eyes had crinkled up when he smiled and those heavenly, heavenly blue eyes.

Not that he'd behaved like a hero, though, leaving her stranded at the airport like that. She sighed, but kept her thoughts to herself. If she mentioned her mystery man to Fiona she'd have to tell her the whole story, and they'd end up even more off topic than they already were.

At least talk of Dr McFarlaine was vaguely relevant to the panto. Meeting the stranger at the airport had been more like something in a dream, surreal and inexplicable. She was starting to wonder if it had even happened. She'd been so distressed at the time, she felt that she could quite easily have dreamed up the whole encounter.

Nevertheless, Eleanor fell asleep that night thinking about her handsome stranger and woke the next morning with a picture of him in her head and a smile on her face.

★　★　★

When Eleanor approached Fiona's young doctor in the street the next day after someone pointed him out to her, she was disappointed. He was kind of good-looking — in the ginger-haired, freckled way Fiona had always liked — but the poor chap was painfully shy. When she asked if he'd consider taking part in the panto he recoiled in horror, his face crimson and stuttered, 'N-n-no t-thank you, I don't think I'd be very good at that.'

His refusal was accompanied by a charming, though self-effacing smile, which made Eleanor start to under-stand what her friend saw in him. He might not be suitable for the part of Prince Charming, but he might just be perfect for Fiona.

Not one to miss an opportunity, Eleanor said: 'Oh, that's a shame. It was my friend Fiona Johnstone who suggested you. She's a nurse,' she added by way of explanation.

'Oh aye, I've met Nurse Johnstone at the hospital a couple of times,' he replied. 'Is she in your pantomime, then?'

Eleanor could see a definite gleam of interest in his eyes at the mention of Fiona.

'Yes, she is. Are you sure I can't convince you to change your mind?' she added innocently.

But it seemed that not even her friend's wild blonde curls and curvy figure could tempt this tall, shy man to get up on a stage.

'I really don't think it would be a good idea,' he said smiling sadly. 'I'd end up missing lots of rehearsals through working late or getting called out to see patients after hours. And I've never been any good at public speaking. I get so tongue-tied, I'd mess up all my lines. But I'll definitely come and see it,' he added enthusiastically, 'you can put me down for a ticket right away.'

Well, that was encouraging at least. It looked as though Doctor McFarlaine was as interested in Fiona as she was in him. Eleanor would certainly have to do whatever she could to help them along.

But it still left her with the problem of no Prince Charming and the performance only a matter of weeks away now! She'd hate to have to cancel at this late date. Her grandparents had asked for her help saving the panto and she wasn't going to give up without a fight.

Still, she was starting to wonder if it was doomed. First there was the issue of a director with severe memory problems, then the pregnant leading lady had to bow out and now the leading man had been knocked out due to injury. What on earth could go wrong next? Was it even safe for the rest of them to carry on? Maybe they'd have to start talking about *Cinderella* as 'The Scottish Panto' in the way actors superstitiously referred to *Macbeth* as 'The Scottish Play'.

What Eleanor needed was a miracle, but as those seemed to be in short supply at the moment she decided the only thing to do was put a notice up in the shop and pub and on the noticeboards outside the church and village hall. *Prince Charming urgently required, apply within* were the words that sprang to mind. But she could imagine how much fun the local wags would have with that one and didn't want to turn herself into the laughing stock of Tullymuir.

Instead, the notices she posted stated the date and times for new auditions for the part of Prince Charming, and asked good-naturedly for 'anyone to come along and have ago'.

She was even wondering whether to have a woman play the part. It was quite a tradition in the theatre to have men playing female roles — like the Ugly Sisters — and women playing the leading man, whether it was Prince Charming or Peter Pan. She'd seen a female Robin Hood once. Maybe she could play the part herself and let one of the other women in the cast be Cinderella?

After several rounds of auditions, which failed to produce a suitable new Prince Charming, Eleanor had almost decided to go with Plan B. But she thought she'd better keep it as a last resort since it wouldn't be popular, certainly not with the younger contingent of local women. If the men in the audience got to admire whatever woman played the part of Cinderella, it seemed only fair for the women to have a handsome man to make their hearts flutter as Prince Charming.

'Well, that's it, then,' Eleanor said to herself as she locked the doors of the village hall and trudged up the hill to her grandparents' house. She must have seen every man in the local area between the ages of eighteen and sixty and there was still no one who fitted the bill.

She reluctantly broke the bad news to her grandparents over dinner that night.

'So, I think I might have to play Prince Charming myself,' she concluded as cheerfully as she could. 'I could ask Fiona or maybe Allison to step in as Cinderella. But if Mrs Moore was confused before, I don't know how she'll cope with this!'

'Hold your horses, love,' her grandfather said, looking towards his wife who gave a brief nod. 'Your grandmother and I might have come up with another solution.'

Eleanor hoped Grandpa wasn't going to volunteer to play the part himself. Much as she loved him he really wasn't Prince Charming material. Maybe he could have pulled it off convincingly when he was forty years younger, but he was in his seventies now.

He also spent so much time underneath cars that he permanently lived in a boiler suit and had hands ingrained with engine oil. On the plus side, she supposed it would mean that Cinders needn't worry about her pumpkin coach breaking down. Wait! Maybe she could re-write the script so that Prince Charming came to the rescue of Cinderella when her coach broke down on the way to the ball?

When that thought came to her, Eleanor knew was getting desperate and starting to clutch at straws. It was true you could get away with quite a lot in a pantomime, but there were limits.

'So what do you think?' her grandfather asked.

'Er, sorry, I didn't hear what you said,' Eleanor admitted, dragging herself back to reality.

'I told you she wasn't paying attention, Nana muttered, pursing her lips.

'I said, we knew you were struggling to find yourself a Prince Charming,' he

141

repeated slowly, 'so your nana and I talked to our friends Andy and Rachel McIntyre and they're going to see if they can convince their son Jim to help out.'

'He'd be absolutely perfect,' Nana said. 'And he might just do it, seeing as we're in a real fix.'

'If he's so perfect, why didn't he didn't come along to any of the auditions?' Eleanor asked warily. She'd been introduced to the grandsons of Nana and Papa's friends before . . . Talking of which if this was their friends' son rather than grandson, surely he'd be too old? Most of their friends had sons in their fifties.

'He just prefers to keep himself to himself,' her grandpa explained.

'And who can blame him?' her nana added.

'That might be a sensible philosophy for life in general, but it doesn't bode well for a leading man,' Eleanor retorted. 'They're usually flamboyant, extrovert, loud and a bit annoying. And to a certain extent, they need to be.'

'Don't you worry about that, love, I'm sure he'll do a grand job,' her grandfather reassured her.

'If he agrees,' her grandmother said.

'Do you know if this Jim character has done any acting before?' Eleanor asked.

'You could say that,' her grandfather said, turning away, but not before Eleanor noticed a distinct twinkle in his eye.

Well, they obviously weren't going to tell her any more, so she'd just have to wait and see.

11

They were halfway through the next rehearsal before Eleanor got to meet the elusive Jim. A rather shamefaced Craig had turned up, hobbling on crutches and offering to read the part of Prince Charming until a replacement was found. He'd heard about all the auditions and was very apologetic about having caused so much trouble.

'Now that I'm up and about it's the least I can do. And you never know, maybe my ankle will heal in record time and I'll be able to play the part after all,' he said optimistically.

But Eleanor noticed Fiona shaking her head in the background, wiggling the fingers of both hands in the air and mouthing 'ten weeks'.

'Don't worry about it, Craig,' Eleanor reassured him. 'I've got someone coming along this evening who might be able to help. And in the meantime, we're all very grateful to you for standing in.'

'Well, sitting in, if you don't mind,' Craig said, grinning at his own joke and settling himself comfortably on the old sofa up on the stage.

'Who have you got coming?' Margaret demanded.

'Andrew hasn't changed his mind, has he?' Fiona whispered, colour suffusing her cheeks.

'No, he hasn't,' Eleanor muttered, before announcing loudly, 'It's the son of my grandparents' friends, the McIntyres. Someone called Jim.'

The atmosphere in the hall changed in an instant. Up until then, everything had been fairly relaxed and casual but suddenly the air felt still and heavy, crackling with anticipation as it did before a storm. A deathly hush came over everyone. Eleanor was tempted to drop a pin just to find out if the saying was true. Then she was engulfed in a wave of noise as

145

everyone started to talk at once.

'Oh aye, young Jimmy will see us right,' Tommy said, sounding whole-heartedly relieved.

'Well, if that is indeed the case, then we've nothing more to worry about,' Margaret pronounced, even managing a smile. 'The show is guaranteed to be a success.'

'We're in safe hands, that's for sure,' Hamish muttered.

'That's one pair of hands I wouldn't mind being in!' Betty said, making some of the other young women giggle.

Eleanor wondered what on earth was going on. Everybody seemed to know something she didn't. She looked round at the cast and saw the men standing a little taller, backs straight and chests thrust out. There was a fair amount of chest thrusting from the women too, along with some surreptitious hair brushing and lipstick retouching. The only person who didn't look too happy was Craig Buchanan.

'Well, I might as well go, then,' he said grumpily, trying to get back up off the sofa.

Eleanor was completely bemused. She was just about to ask Fiona why everyone was behaving so strangely when the hall door banged open.

It was a wild day, windy and wet, and the motorbike courier who stepped into the hall dressed from head to toe in black leather stood dripping on the mat. Eleanor was used to seeing couriers in London all the time, but hadn't expected to see one up here in the Highlands.

Strangely, he didn't seem to be carrying anything to deliver. Eleanor went forward to find out who he was looking for. Maybe he was lost and needed directions. By the time she'd climbed off the stage and walked to the front of the hall he'd removed his leather jacket and helmet.

'Can I help you?' she asked. 'Are you lost?'

'If this is the rehearsal for *Cinderella*,

then I'm not lost,' a familiar softly-spoken voice said.

The man turned round and Eleanor gasped. It was the stranger from the airport! And he was standing in front of her, looking large as life and twice as gorgeous. She opened and closed her mouth but no words came out.

'And as I understand it, I'm here to help you he added, when she didn't speak.

Eleanor just had time to register that he sounded none too pleased about it when everything clicked into place. The 'Jim' her grandpa had talked about and the 'young Jimmy' Tommy had been relieved to have coming to help was none other than Hollywood legend James McIntyre. Now all the women's primping and preening made perfect sense.

'It's you!' Eleanor exclaimed. 'From the airport.' She wondered how on earth she hadn't recognised him at the time. He was a major Hollywood film star, for heaven's sake, and she'd seen him in half a dozen movies at least.

'You're James McIntyre,' she added accusingly.

A glimmer of a smile lit up his blue eyes. 'I know,' he said, 'but thanks for reminding me.'

And with that they were surrounded by the rest of the cast, so that in the midst of the crowd Eleanor hoped her crimson cheeks would go unnoticed.

'Hey, Jimmy, good to see you,' Tommy said, shaking hands with him.

'Aye, we thought we were sunk until you got here,' Hamish added.

Eleanor glanced at him sharply. *Thanks a bunch*, she thought. It was galling to know that was what people had really been thinking. All the time she she'd been under the impression she was doing quite a good job — in the circumstances — and they obviously thought the exact opposite.

Now she knew exactly how poor Katie Moore must have felt that night she walked in on them all discussing her. Only that incident had been mercifully wiped from Katie's memory, while Eleanor would just have to live with her own humiliation.

Oh no, she thought, *talking of humiliation* . . . James McIntyre may well know all about her London show being a flop. She felt her heart start to beat harder and faster. Was he about to commiserate with her about it and show her up in front of everyone? Was there any chance he might not know about it?

No such luck. He and Brandon Stone were arch rivals, so he was bound to keep tabs on what Brandon was up to.

While all these thoughts were flitting round Eleanor's brain, she watched James McIntyre shaking hands with everyone, pausing to say a word or two to each person and generally charming the entire cast. When he got to Mrs Moore, he stooped to kiss her cheek.

'Hello Katie, you probably don't recognise me with this daft haircut, I barely recognise myself sometimes, but it's me all right — Jim McIntyre.'

Natalia nodded at him approvingly.

'Little Jimmy McIntyre! I'd know you anywhere dear,' she said, giving him a hug. 'I hear you've been doing quite well for yourself recently.'

James took this massive understatement and the use of his childhood nickname in his stride.

'Not bad at all, Katie,' he replied. 'And a lot of that is down to you. So when Mum and Dad heard you were short a Prince Charming for your panto they sent me over to ask if I could help. They also sent their love.'

'I'm very happy to accept both the love and the help,' Katie replied. 'As you can see our current Prince Charming has had a wee accident,' she added, nodding towards Craig.

James McIntyre managed not to laugh when he saw Craig standing on the stage, wobbling on his crutches and glowering at him. But his eyes were sparkling with laughter as he walked past Eleanor to climb onto the stage.

'I'm sorry you're out of the running.

No hard feelings, man,' he said, patting Craig on the back. 'I hear you're quite the sportsman, so I take it you got injured playing rugby or skiing?'

Craig flushed as there were a few sniggers from round the hall.

'Actually, I was out shooting and got my foot stuck in a rabbit hole,' he admitted sheepishly.

'I did the same thing myself once,' James replied, neglecting to mention that he'd been six years old at the time.

Craig grinned and Eleanor marvelled at how easily James had managed to appease and even befriend the person he was replacing. She knew for a fact that Betty hadn't forgiven her, despite their very fake, theatrical showdown and handshake. *How on earth did he do it?* she wondered. He made it look so effortless, too. It was sickening! And she still hadn't forgiven him for abandoning her at the airport.

Worst of all, here she was doomed to work with yet another Hollywood actor after vowing never do so again as long as she lived. She sighed. It was going to be a long evening.

* * *

After James had finished doing the rounds, he politely stepped back and waited to be told what to do.

Eleanor, the beautiful girl from the airport who'd been occupying his mind far too much lately, thrust a script in his hand with a scowl on her face. He felt really bad for leaving her at the airport without a ride, especially as he now knew she wasn't a stalker at all. What a big-headed idiot he was, assuming it had been all about him! He really needed to spend more time here at home with his parents and other normal people, instead of surrounded by Hollywood luvvies.

That was one of the reasons why he'd allowed his parents to talk him into taking on the part of Prince Charming in the Christmas panto. Usually he kept a low profile when he was back at

153

home. But as his dad pointed out, who on earth would have any interest in a pantomime being performed in a tiny village in the Scottish Highlands?

Besides, Mrs Moore needed his help and he'd do anything for her. She used to run an after-school drama club, which was what got him interested in acting in the first place.

But if he was honest, his real reason for coming tonight was to see the girl from the airport again. He'd tried to put her out of his mind but it hadn't worked, not even when he'd thought she was a stalker.

Let's face it, she was the kind of woman most men would be thrilled to be stalked by. She was gorgeous to look at with her long, wavy auburn hair, light brown eyes and creamy skin. But he'd met enough women who were gorgeous on the outside, and pure poison underneath, to be wary of looks like that.

It was the sweetness in her smile, the way she'd made him laugh and the fun they'd had talking together that made him desperate to see her again. She'd been so easy to talk to. He couldn't remember the last time he'd enjoyed himself as much, had felt so relaxed, so un-judged.

He'd sat beside her in the airport hoping the plane would be delayed forever so he could talk to her all night. And yes; she'd also made his heart beat harder and faster than his daily five-mile run did. She'd been perfect, and it was a long time since he'd thought that about anyone. Which was why he'd been so furious when she said she was going to Tullymuir. It was too much of a coincidence for her to be going to the same remote Scottish village as he was himself.

Only, as he later found out, it hadn't been too much of a coincidence after all. The problem was, James wasn't a great believer in coincidences. More often than not — in Hollywood at least — what looked like a coincidence turned out to be a well planned and carefully thought-out strategy. So one minute he'd had his ideal woman at his side; the next it seemed she'd turned into someone who was just the same as everyone else.

Extreme disappointment on top of total exhaustion had made him jump to the wrong conclusion and he'd behaved appallingly.

On the journey home he'd nearly turned back several times. He hadn't calmed down completely until he arrived at his parents' house, wishing with all his heart that he hadn't just walked away from the woman he felt might just be the one.

Then a few weeks later, his parents explained how the Christies' granddaughter — a young woman called Eleanor — was trying single-handedly to keep the Tullymuir Dramatic Society panto going and he'd finally put two and two together. The woman he'd met at the airport really *had* been trying to get to Tullymuir. He felt deeply ashamed of his behaviour and wished he'd acted on his instincts and gone back for her.

How on earth did she get to Tullymuir without a hire car? A taxi would have cost a fortune. The name Eleanor Christie sounded familiar, too. Wasn't there a British actress of that name?

He did an online search and images of the beautiful woman he'd half fallen in love with at the airport popped up on his phone. He gazed hungrily at the tiny screen and dragged his eyes away from her beautiful face long enough to read the accompanying biography. She'd been a big success on the London stage for a number of years and had recently branched out into directing.

He hoped she wasn't the amazing female director his friend Brandon had been banging on about — the one who'd given him a chance when no one else would, as a result of which he'd discovered a talent for comedy he never knew he had. Brandon had phoned to tell James all about it — how the play he was currently in was a great success, how the critics were raving about it and how it was sold out for months ahead.

The media thought James and Brandon were arch rivals, an image they'd carefully cultivated. In reality, they were the best of friends. In the mad whirl of Hollywood each had been surprised but delighted to find a like-minded soul. They were both small-town boys who'd suddenly made it big. Even though one was from a small village in the Scottish Highlands and the other came from a one-horse town in Minnesota, they felt like kindred spirits. Brandon was drinking too much and James was partying too hard in a desperate attempt to look as though they fitted in. It was a relief to find someone in the same position.

They started spending time together, shooting pool and playing video games. But when a few sly comments started appearing in the media about their 'friendship' and how close they seemed to be, their agents suggested a manufactured bust-up over some young actress. It worked, but left them both friendless again.

Still, when things got really bad — or good — they'd chat over the internet or on the phone to keep themselves sane and grounded. Brandon had rung from London, elated with his success on the stage, but concerned about the director who'd disappeared after opening night leaving only her mobile phone behind. After reading about her on the internet, James was hoping against hope that Eleanor — *his* Eleanor — wasn't the same woman Brandon seemed so desperate to find.

He hadn't said as much, but James suspected his friend had fallen in love with the missing director. He was certainly searching everywhere for her. If it turned out to be Eleanor, where did that leave them? Should one of them step aside for the sake of his friend's happiness?

James decided to watch Eleanor

closely during the rehearsal. He'd been in this game long enough to already have an idea of how things stood. He could sense undercurrents of discontent and confusion and could see from the start that Eleanor was trying to organise this rag-tag group into a cohesive cast, without making it too obvious. What was she up to?

She kept deferring to Katie Moore, asking her opinion, using the lightest of touches but all the time pulling the whole thing together by sheer force of will. She certainly knew what she was doing. But as an experienced actress she would do; it didn't mean she was Brandon's missing director. And then he stopped trying to work things out, he stopped thinking at all, when Eleanor switched from organising to acting.

James was spellbound; she was totally mesmerising. Even without the costumes, sets and lighting she lit up the stage. Even with amateur actors around her fluffing their lines and moving like wooden marionettes, Eleanor shone.

She made him believe she was the poor downtrodden Cinderella. He wanted to punch her Wicked Stepmother and Ugly Sisters, rescue her from her world of drudgery amongst the ashes and dirty dishes and ride away with her on his white horse. He knew he was being ridiculous, he didn't even have a white horse — only a black motorbike.

'Er, James, it's your line,' Eleanor said, turning back from being Cinderella into herself again. 'It's the bit in the palace where the Grand Duke is trying to convince you to hold a ball so you can find a princess to marry.'

James swallowed hard and flipped through his script to the right page. *Pull yourself together, man*, he said to himself. *You're meant to be the professional actor here.*

He forced himself to concentrate and managed to get through the rest of the rehearsal. But he was profoundly relieved not to have to act a scene with Eleanor. They stopped long before the ball. He didn't know how he'd manage to hold her in his arms as they danced without pulling her close and kissing her, how he'd look into her eyes and say the words on the script instead of telling her what was in his heart.

And then, suddenly, the rehearsal was over. Where had the time gone? He'd never known a rehearsal to fly by so quickly. He felt elated and disappointed at the same time. Relieved to have survived the evening without giving himself away, thrilled to be in Eleanor's company again but sad to have to say goodnight and walk away from her. In fact . . .

'Anyone for a drink at The Old Thistle?' he asked, hopefully, when they were all putting chairs away and tidying the hall to leave it ready for the church jumble sale the next day.

'That's a great idea.'

'We usually just go straight home afterwards.'

'I can't make it — got to get back to the kids.'

James heard the various comments

floating around him, but they didn't really register. It was Eleanor's response he was waiting for. He turned to look at her but she wasn't paying any attention at all, her eyes were turned to the stage.

He followed her line of vision and his heart sank. She was smiling tenderly as she watched Craig Buchanan being helped up from the old saggy sofa he was sitting on.

James's heart sank. The guy might be a total klutz but there was no denying he was good-looking and if there was one thing a woman loved, it was an injured man. It seemed to bring out the nurturer in them.

It wasn't unusual for the male and female leads to have a bit of a fling. Sometimes even actors found it difficult to tell the difference between acting and real life. To be convincingly in love with your leading lady you had to pretend you really were in love with her, and pretence could all too easily turn to reality.

James felt a spark of hope. Maybe

now he was Prince Charming, Eleanor would fall for him?

But when she rather coldly declined his reiterated offer of a drink, his hopes were dashed.

12

Eleanor was furious with James McIntyre. She didn't know what was annoying her more: the fact he hadn't let on who he was at the airport; the way he'd left her there with no way of getting home — which she hadn't forgiven him for; how he'd turned up at yesterday's rehearsal and charmed everyone including Craig; or the fact that he was actually a really good actor, not just another Hollywood movie star like Brandon Stone.

She should of course be pleased to find out he was such a good actor, it meant that between the two of them they might just be able to save the pantomime and maybe even get TADS back on track. But she wasn't pleased at all. She didn't want to be beholden to him and she certainly didn't want to have to work closely with him for the next four weeks.

Eleanor had made very sure they didn't have to rehearse any scenes together last night. She knew that if they had, she'd have given herself away completely. She remembered all too clearly the moment at the airport when they'd shaken hands and a jolt of electricity had coursed through her body. If James McIntyre took her in his arms, she thought her legs might actually give way. But she couldn't put it off forever. Sooner or later they'd have to rehearse their scenes, she'd have to dance with him, put her hand on his shoulder and feel his arm around her waist, look up into those gorgeous blue eyes . . . Eleanor's hand shook and a trickle of ash fell from the shovel she was holding.

Of course it did explain why she hadn't recognised him at the airport: real actors transformed themselves into the characters they played. She'd known actresses who were capable of looking beautiful in one role and quite plain in another. Obviously, some of that was down to make-up and costume, but mostly it was what the actor drew from inside themselves.

Eleanor had watched movies with James McIntyre in them, from costume dramas to science fiction blockbusters and each time he'd been completely different. He'd spoken with a clipped BBC English accent, a southern American drawl, a Glaswegian growl and everything in between. But his real voice, that soft Scottish accent she'd heard at the airport, and his real personality which she'd glimpsed there as well, had never appeared on any screen. No wonder she hadn't recognised him.

But he could have had the decency to tell her who he was, instead of letting her make a complete fool of herself? She gulped down angry tears. What was most annoying of all was that she'd really liked him — more than just liked, if she was being honest.

Eleanor brushed the fireplace more

vigorously than she'd intended and a waft of ashes drifted up and made her sneeze. For a moment she was distracted from her thoughts about James. She loved her grandparents' fire and could literally spend hours gazing into the flames. Wood smoke was one of her favourite smells and when she had a house of her own some day, she fully intended to have a proper fireplace too. But she didn't enjoy the daily task of emptying out the burnt ashes and sweeping the fireplace clean ready for that night's fire.

She lifted the shovel loaded with last night's cold ashes on it and was carefully carrying it through the lounge to take it outside into the garden when her grandmother called her name.

'Ella, where are you? Jim is here to see you.'

Eleanor's hand shook and she spilled the ashes down her jeans and onto the carpet.

She dashed back to the fireplace and hastily thrust the shovel back into it

— she'd have to sweep it up again later. She was down on her hands and knees trying to rub the worst of the mess from her nana's best carpet when the door opened and Janet walked in, closely followed by James McIntyre.

'What on earth are you doing?' Janet asked.

'You made me jump when you shouted for me just now and I spilled some ashes,' Eleanor admitted shame-facedly.

She heard a soft laugh.

'Very appropriate for someone play-ing the part of Cinderella,' James teased.

Eleanor glared at him.

'I don't know about that,' her grandmother said, tutting over the mess, 'but it isn't doing my carpet any good.'

'Sorry, Nana.' Eleanor felt ten years old again.

'As a matter of fact, I've come to say sorry myself,' James quickly interjected.

Janet looked from one to the other

and said, with unusual tact, that she'd just go and make some tea.

When the door closed behind her, James didn't immediately say anything. There was an awkward silence as they both looked at each other, then looked away. Eventually their eyes met again.

'I wanted to apologise for my behaviour at the airport,' he said, in a rush. 'I feel really bad for leaving you there that night.'

'And so you should!' Eleanor retorted, determined not to make it easy for him. 'There were no hire cars available at all. I had to make other arrangements.'

'Other arrangements?' he asked, obviously curious to know how she'd managed to. get from Inverness Airport to Tullymuir so late at night.

'Never you mind,' she said. She wasn't going to let him off the hook so easily. 'Why did you leave me there? One minute you were offering to drive me to John O' Groats, the next you were out of the door before I could say goodbye.'

'I know it sounds ridiculous,' he replied, 'but the truth is, when you said you were going to Tullymuir I thought you were only saying that because it's where I was going. I thought you might be stalking me.'

Now it was his turn to look shamefaced.

'Stalking you!' Eleanor said. 'You arrogant — '

'I know, and I'm sorry, but it's happened to me before.'

'Oh, poor you! Well, for your information I had no idea who you were!' Eleanor retorted, hoping to wound his pride. 'I knew you had to be a celebrity of some kind, but I thought you might be out of a boy band or something.'

'A *boy band*?' James asked incredulously.

'Yes, a boy band.' She was enjoying his offended look. 'Imagine! The great James McIntyre and I didn't even recognise you, how silly of me!'

James looked up, but instead of being angry she saw something like hope in his eyes.

'I didn't think you knew who I was,' he said, smiling.

'So why didn't you tell me?' she demanded. 'I feel like such a fool.'

When she raised her eyes he was standing very close.

'You're not a fool,' he said gently. 'And I wasn't making fun of you, just enjoying being liked for myself for once. Because you did seem to like me — at the time.'

That was a serious understatement. Eleanor swallowed. She was finding it hard to concentrate. James was so close she could feel the heat coming from his body, and when he spoke, his warm breath tickled her skin. She shivered.

'You must know what it's like,' he went on, when she didn't speak. 'You're a successful actor too. Oh yes, I know all about you, Eleanor Christie. I read all about your success on the London stage. So you know exactly what I'm talking about. When people know who you are, you're never quite sure whether it's you they like or one of the characters you've played, or worse still, whether they just want you to introduce them to someone who can help their career.'

Eleanor did know what he meant, though she was in a completely different league success-wise. But before she could answer, Janet came in carrying a heavy tea tray.

They sprang apart like guilty teenagers and James gallantly took the tray from her nana. She didn't join them, making some excuse about having to take a cake out of the oven shortly.

They sat awkwardly on the sofa, side by side. For something to do, Eleanor reached for the teapot and poured them both a cup.

'I just wanted a lift home,' Eleanor said eventually, taking a sip of tea.

'I know that now,' James replied. 'And I really am sorry. Though you might not have been so keen if you'd known I was offering you a lift on my bike, rather than in a car,' he added, with a flash of the gorgeous smile she remembered from the airport.

Eleanor thought about the biker's leathers he was wearing when he arrived at the rehearsal last night, and recalled the strange comment he'd made at the airport about whether her rucksack was all the luggage she had. It all started to make sense. She gave a reluctant smile.

'It was tipping it down that night, so maybe I was better off in a car than on the back of a motorbike,' she said, even though she knew it wasn't true. She'd have been far happier with her arms wrapped around James, snuggling into his back, even if it had been coming down in torrents.

'So you managed to get a lift, then?' he asked, seeming genuinely concerned. 'I had visions of you sleeping in the airport.'

Eleanor decided to put him out of his

misery. She relented and told him how the kind man from the car hire desk had lent her their staff car.

'So tell me what's going on with this panto then,' he said, helping himself to one of Janet's freshly baked biscuits and settling himself more comfortably on the sofa. 'There seemed to be more going on last night than just a straightforward rehearsal.'

'Only if you tell me why you lied to Katie about being happy to help out,' she retorted.

'What makes you think I'm not happy to help?' he asked, nearly choking on his biscuit.

'I could hear it in your voice when you first arrived,' Eleanor replied. 'But of course that was before you went into full schmooze mode and charmed the pants off everyone.'

Eleanor felt her face redden. She wished she hadn't used that phrase. Thinking about James and underwear at the same time was making her feel all hot and bothered.

He raised an eloquent eyebrow and smiled, but it was her other phrase he latched onto.

'Full schmooze mode?' he demanded, pretending to be offended.

'You know what I mean,' Eleanor said. 'One minute you were all snooty. What was it you said? Oh yes, I quote. 'As I understand it, I'm here to help you.'

James grimaced. 'Did I really say that?'

'Yes, you did,' Eleanor replied. 'You sounded like something out of Jane Austen.'

'Sorry,' he said. 'I seem to be spending a lot of my time apologising to you, don't I?'

'Quite right too!' she said. 'Now stop changing the subject. Why don't you want to help with the panto? I thought maybe you considered it beneath you, but from talking to you this morning I don't think that's the case.'

'Of course not!' he exclaimed. 'It's just that when I'm at home I try to avoid acting altogether. I stick to normal, everyday things like taking the trash out, helping my parents round the house and going to the pub. It helps me get my feet back on the ground.'

'Taking out the trash?' Eleanor teased. 'Don't you mean the rubbish? I think you've spent too long in Hollywood.'

'Far too long,' James answered seriously.

'Well, if you think you can bear to join us, we really could use your help,' Eleanor admitted. 'There have been times when I've wondered if this show is actually doomed.' She went on to explain about Katie Moore's memory problem, Betty McCardle's pregnancy, the stolen items and Craig's accident.

'You certainly seem to have had more than your fair share of bad luck,' he concluded. 'But if it's any consolation, that should mean everything goes really well for the actual performances. At least, that's been my experience in the theatre.'

'You're right,' Eleanor said, 'I hadn't thought of that. And I promise I'll help you to keep your feet on the ground.'

'I'm going to hold you to that,' James said, his eyes locking onto hers and his words loaded with meaning. Eleanor swallowed and looked away. She tried to make light of it.

'Of course,' she said. 'Even if everyone else kowtows to you and treats you like royalty, I promise I won't.'

'Not even when I'm playing Prince Charming?'

'Not even then,' she replied, with a smile.

'And what about your other Prince Charming?' he asked cautiously.

'What, Craig? I'm sure he's resigned himself to his fate by now. Despite all his wishful thinking, even he must realise Prince Charming can't sweep Cinderella off her feet at the ball while dancing on crutches. And you certainly seemed to win him over last night. In fact I don't think either of us will have to worry about him any more,' she added, an odd little smile on her lips.

When she saw the puzzled look on James's face she explained, 'He had a bit of a thing for me. But after the look he gave Natalia last night, I think we can safely say he's moved on! I don't know if you've noticed, but when Natalia smiles her face is utterly transformed and she becomes quite beautiful. I was lucky enough to witness the moment last night when she turned that amazing smile on Craig for the first time. He was completely bowled over. In fact, if he hadn't had his crutches to lean on I think he'd have fallen down!'

James felt his heart soar in his chest. So that's why Eleanor had been smiling while she gazed at Craig on the stage last night. She wasn't in love with him after all. James felt as though all his Christmases had come at once.

13

The next few weeks passed in a golden glow for Eleanor. With James on board, everything started going far more smoothly with the panto.

The entire cast were on best behaviour when he was around. Everyone made a concerted effort to learn their lines and remember their cues and far fewer mistakes were made, now that everyone was trying desperately to impress him.

And if anyone should happen to make a mistake, James made light of it, usually relating a story about something similar he'd done himself to make them feel better. There was a lot more laughter and fun in the air and Eleanor could feel the stress slowly slipping away.

James certainly had a way with people, especially women — and not just the younger ones. These days Margaret Reid was smiling so much more, she actually had to put on her old flinty expression when she was playing the Wicked Stepmother. And Eleanor nearly laughed aloud when she heard Margaret giving Moira some genuine encouragement, instead of terrifying her with her usual criticisms. Moira had blossomed, too — she seemed to be transforming into a Fairy Godmother like the one in the Disney film before Eleanor's eyes. Gone was her permanently worried expression, and instead her round face was all smiles.

Even Mrs Moore's memory seemed less erratic, so that Eleanor almost began to wonder if her old teacher had not been as bad as she'd feared. But Fiona explained that Katie's improvement made perfect sense: with Eleanor and James running the show, she wasn't under as much pressure and so was far less muddled and distressed.

As for Natalia, the woman was worth her weight in gold. Under her direction, the sets and costumes were coming on apace, the props were dusted, labelled and numbered so they were easy to find and the hall was always immaculately clean. She managed to do all of that while keeping a watchful eye on Mrs Moore and taking care of Craig and his dodgy ankle too.

After each rehearsal, the entire cast retreated to The Old Thistle to talk it over, discuss any issues and make suggestions for improvements. It didn't escape Eleanor's notice that James was always the first to stand a round of drinks. A feeling of genuine camaraderie was springing up between them all, so that Eleanor wasn't too surprised when she bumped into members of the cast socialising outside of rehearsals.

She was particularly pleased to find Betty McCardle helping Mrs Moore with her shopping one morning and thought the better of her for it. Betty seemed to have reconciled herself to the idea of losing the starring role in *Cinderella* and had surprised everyone by continuing to turn up at rehearsals to help out.

Craig was doing the same and had become remarkably adept at moving around on his crutches, though his injury was improving every day thanks to Natalia's loving care. So there were always willing volunteers to act as prompt in case anyone forgot their lines, to stand in if anyone was missing or just running late, or even simply to run errands and carry messages.

Best of all, Eleanor was delighted to find that James really had meant what he'd said. He genuinely wanted to get back to real life, to be normal and treated the same as everyone else.

If they turned up and found the hall filled with chairs, James would help to stack and move them. When Natalia suggested a Sunday afternoon painting party to get the sets finished, he turned up in an old pair of paint-spattered jeans and T-shirt ready to muck in. He wasn't much of a painter, which came as a relief to Eleanor who'd started to wonder if there was anything he couldn't do. But he mixed emulsion, refilled buckets, made endless teas and coffees and even popped to the fish and chip shop in the evening when they were all tired and hungry.

Without seeming to push himself forward in anyway, James made himself indispensable and Eleanor felt as though a huge burden had been lifted from her shoulders. She got so used to asking for his help and advice that she wondered how she'd managed before he came along.

He made none of the outlandish demands Eleanor was used to after working with famous actors over the years. There were no special requests for sparking mineral water, or diva-ish tantrums over having to share a dressing room — which was just as well since the Tullymuir Village Hall didn't run to dressing rooms at all.

When the time came to try on their costumes, the women used the large committee room near the entrance and the men made do with the smaller area to the side of the stage where the props and costumes were stored. The two wags, Tommy and Hamish, did try to argue the case for being allowed to change in the committee room too, as they were playing the Ugly Sisters and wearing women's clothes.

But even though James had dropped his Hollywood persona completely, his outstanding acting abilities were still there for all to see. And when he changed into his Prince Charming costume so that Jacqui could make a few adjustments, Eleanor could only gaze in open admiration while she heard gasps and sighs coming from all the female members of the cast.

Never had the old-fashioned navy military jacket with its brass buttons and gold epaulettes looked so good. It had been wheeled out for countless productions to represent everything from soldiers and statesmen to lords and princes. Now, standing in the middle of the Tullymuir Village Hall in that well-worn jacket, James McIntyre looked like the embodiment of Prince Charming. He was every woman's fantasy of the handsome prince who would one day come and rescue her.

James held out his hand to Eleanor and spoke the words from the script.

'*May I have the pleasure of this dance?*' he asked, smiling down at her.

Eleanor caught her breath, gave him her hand and allowed herself to be swept round the stage to the strains of Tchaikovsky's *Sleeping Beauty Waltz*. Tommy had pointed out that the music belonged to a different fairy tale altogether but in the end they'd all agreed that though some people would recognise the tune, they probably wouldn't remember what it was called. Besides, it was perfect for the ball scene.

At first Eleanor felt very proud and extremely fortunate to be the one who got to stand beside this handsome man, to take his hand and be swirled round the pretend ballroom. But she forgot all about that, because as soon as she was in James's arms she felt as though she really was Cinderella. She didn't have to act at all.

She could feel herself drowning in his gorgeous blue eyes, felt enveloped by the sweetness of his smile, and knew by the thudding of her heart that his lips were just a few tantalising inches away. He was her whole world, there was nothing and no one else.

Out of the corner of her eye she could swear she caught a glimpse of a sparkling glass chandelier above their heads, and the long red swagged curtains and huge glass doors looked real, not painted onto a backdrop. Somehow she knew that if only she could walk out of those doors they would lead her down a flight of shallow stone steps into a garden filled with winding paths, statues and rose bushes. There would be fountains and fireworks and . . .

When the music and dancing stopped, it was a shock to find herself back on the stage of the village hall.

'That's not quite right, Eleanor,' Margaret Reid's officious voice said, intruding into her wonderful daydream and bringing her harshly back to reality. 'More, like this. Here, let me show you,' Margaret went on, eagerly taking Eleanor's place to show her how to waltz properly.

Eleanor knew she should feel grateful to the older woman for teaching her the proper steps and correcting her mistakes, but she couldn't help wondering whether Margaret wasn't just using it as an excuse to dance with James herself.

Eleanor tried to concentrate, to watch Margaret and follow the steps carefully but she felt sick with disappointment. She wanted to go back to being Cinderella so she could stumble down the stairs, lose her glass slipper and have James McIntyre — or rather, Prince Charming — come looking for her. She felt cheated of her happy ending.

Her only consolation was seeing her

own disappointment mirrored on James's face, though he quickly hid it with a polite smile. She couldn't help noticing that his eyes were drawn to hers over the top of Margaret's head as they danced.

Eleanor swallowed hard and tried to trample down her feelings. She'd seen too many leading ladies fall for their leading men with disastrous results. It could be hard to resist, especially when there was a real chemistry between them, as there seemed to be with her and James. But she knew it could be the kiss of death for a production.

The leads would fall in love on stage and mistakenly think they had in real life too. Then they'd start going out and discover that their on-stage personae and real-life personalities were completely different and incompatible. They'd argue, maybe even split up — and end up having to play love scenes together while glaring at each other and spitting out their declarations of love between gritted teeth.

So even though she found James incredibly attractive, very much enjoyed his company and had started to rely on his wide experience and good sense, there was no way she was going to allow herself to fall in love with him.

At least . . . she wouldn't admit she had until after the show was over. Eleanor sighed under cover of the music. She knew that by then it would be too late; she'd be heading back down to London and James would be off to LA again to start on his next movie. When the show was over, both her opportunity and James would be gone.

★ ★ ★

What made it even harder to resist the gorgeous James was the fact that love seemed to be in the air. Popping into The Old Thistle one lunchtime to get her grandfather a bottle of his favourite beer to go with dinner, she noticed Craig and Natalia in the snug, gazing at each other adoringly.

And on a night out in Inverbruin with her grandparents to celebrate their wedding anniversary she spotted Fiona and Dr McFarlaine sitting in the window of the Italian restaurant they'd been heading for. The couple were talking and sharing a bottle of wine, and just as Eleanor walked past she saw her friend's face light up with laughter and happiness. She quickly hurried her grandparents on and suggested they try the new bistro everyone had been raving about.

Even the usually erratic Scottish weather seemed to be co-operating for a change so that the lovers could enjoy long rambles in the hills without the need for raincoats and umbrellas. The golden days of October seemed reluctant to end and the weather stayed unseasonably dry and mild right into November, when the frosts arrived, transforming everything into a winter wonderland. But Eleanor steadfastly refused all James's offers of walks, dinner, trips to the cinema in

Inverbruin, even lunch at the pub unless there were other people going along too. She simply didn't trust herself to be alone with him. He seemed disappointed by her constant refusals, but she was adamant.

She hoped he hadn't guessed the real reason behind them: she was afraid that if she was alone with him she'd fall head over heels in love with him. She was doing a very good job of resisting him, until the day she bumped into him on one of her long rambles in the hills.

Afterwards she wondered whether his tale of taking a walk to clear his head was true, or whether he'd been been hanging around waiting for her. After all, everyone knew she loved long walks in the hills, breathing in the pure, clean air which now had a bit of a bite to it.

Eleanor hugged her jacket closer as she rounded a bend and felt the full force of the wind. Sitting on an outcrop of rock, looking freezing and thoroughly miserable, was James McIntyre.

'What are you doing out here?' she asked.

'Oh, I was just taking a walk to clear my head,' he replied, jumping up.

Even though he was a good actor, she wasn't convinced. He wore normal shoes, not walking boots and looked blue with cold rather than flushed with exertion. He looked very much like someone who'd been sitting waiting, not walking.

'But I'm glad to have bumped into you,' he said. 'I get the feeling you've been avoiding me and I wanted to know why. Have I done something to annoy you?'

'No, of course you haven't,' Eleanor answered. 'And I haven't been avoiding you,' she lied.

He raised an eyebrow.

'Let's walk while we talk,' Eleanor suggested. 'It's too cold to stand still.'

It also meant she didn't have to face him as they talked, which should make things a little easier. But James spoiled her plan by linking his arm with hers and drawing her as close to his side as possible. That made it much harder for Eleanor to concentrate. As they marched along, she looked down at their feet and noticed they were walking in perfect time like people tied together in a three-legged race.

'So, if I haven't annoyed you, why are you avoiding me?' James asked, his breath leaving visible puffs in the air. He obviously wasn't going to let the matter rest.

'I'm not,' Eleanor reiterated. 'I just don't think it's a good idea for us to get too close. I'm trying to behave professionally.'

'Don't get me wrong,' James said. 'I'm not saying I don't take my role as Prince Charming seriously.' He rather spoiled the effect of his words by giving a huge grin. 'No really, I do,' he said. 'When I act I try to give a hundred per cent, whatever the role or the production. But this isn't the West End, Eleanor, and it's certainly not Hollywood. It's a local panto, for heaven's sake! I think we can afford to lighten up and enjoy ourselves. It's meant to be a bit of fun, both for the audience and the actors. Why are you taking it so seriously?'

'I like to do a good job too,' Eleanor replied. 'You're not the only one who gives a hundred per cent you know.'

'No, I'm not buying it. There's more to it than that,' James persisted. 'It's almost as though you're terrified it's going to go wrong. Why?'

'I am not!' Eleanor retorted, a little too vehemently.

James stepped in front of her.

'What is it, Ella?' he asked gently.

Hearing him call her Ella — the diminutive only used by her grandparents and her closest friends — was the final straw. Eleanor burst into tears. She found herself wrapped in James's arms being shushed and comforted. She felt him stroke her hair and back and she leaned gratefully against his chest until the sobs subsided. Then she stepped back, blew her nose and sighed.

'I suppose I'll have to come clean,' she said, with a groan. 'Though you're not going to think I'm such a serious professional after you hear what happened.'

But when she looked up into his eyes, she saw only kindness and compassion. Maybe she could tell him her secret after all?

'This sounds like a conversation that needs to be had over hot chocolate and cookies. My parents' house is just over that hill — and I make a mean hot chocolate,' he added persuasively.

'But we can't just land in on your parents,' Eleanor objected. She didn't add that her confession was for his ears only.

'Actually, they're not at home at the moment,' he replied, trying to look innocent and failing miserably. 'They've gone to visit my brother today and won't be back until tea time.'

'So we'd be alone,' Eleanor said guardedly.

'Apart from Rupert and Winnie.'

'Who are they?' she asked.

'Mum and Dad's dogs,' he admitted with a rueful smile. 'I'm not sure why, but my mother always seems to name our dogs after fictional bears. The one we had when I was growing up was called Paddington.'

Eleanor smiled but shook her head.

'I don't think that's a good idea.'

'What, naming dogs after fictional bears? I'm joking! How about if I promise to be a perfect gentleman? Sure and Steadfast!' he said, standing to attention and saluting.

'What's that about?' Eleanor asked, delaying the moment when she had to give him an answer.

'I was in the Boys' Brigade for years, it's the Scottish equivalent of the Scouts. And you have my word I won't lay a finger on you from the moment you step in the door until the moment you leave. Unless of course you want me to,' he added with a wicked smile.

Eleanor gave an involuntary shiver. She didn't like to admit that was the very reason she didn't want to be alone with him — the fact that she may very well want him to! It was herself she didn't trust, not him. She was finding it difficult enough to resist him as it was.

'Come on!' he said cheerfully, taking her arm again. 'What's the worst that can happen?'

The temptation was too great. Eleanor agreed. What *was* the worst that could happen?

I could fall in love with you, she answered silently, inside her head.

14

James's parents' house turned out to be a modest, whitewashed farmhouse, which he told her had recently been completely renovated and modernised. Eleanor wondered whether that was a result of his ongoing success in Hollywood, but he didn't say.

When they stepped inside it felt deliciously warm and they were given an enthusiastic welcome by Rupert and Winnie. She managed to disentangle herself from her new furry friends, who were big and bouncy and suited their bear-like names, and looked around with interest while James hung up her coat. She followed him through to the kitchen, admiring her surroundings as she went.

This was Eleanor's idea of a perfect home, a combination of old and new. There were fireplaces and an impressive staircase, but clean, modern lines and big picture windows for admiring the views. Eleanor sat in the kitchen at a kind of breakfast bar looking out over the garden, while James bustled about.

The dogs had settled at her feet so she was free to observe her host at her leisure. He obviously knew his way around a kitchen, which was a nice change after her previous boyfriend Owen, who'd struggled to put a tea bag into a mug. Still, she was surprised to see James walk past the microwave and start opening cupboards to pull out pans and ingredients. Surely all he needed was milk and cocoa powder?

She watched as he set two gleaming copper pans on the hob of the high-tech looking range.

'What on earth are you doing? I thought you were making hot chocolate, not a three-course meal!' Eleanor said, as still more ingredients were dragged out.

'I am making hot chocolate. Look

and learn, young apprentice, look and learn.'

James's idea of hot chocolate was very different from her own and soon Eleanor found herself drawn to the hob to see what was going on. He produced a solid block of chocolate about the size and weight of a large bar of soap and asked her to grate some into the glass bowl he'd perched on top of one of the copper pots which was simmering away.

While the chocolate melted she watched him warming milk in the other pan, infusing it with a cinnamon stick and part of a vanilla bean pod before adding a dash of chilli powder and a pinch of salt. He gave her a running commentary, reminding her of Jamie Oliver in full flight.

Eleanor wished she hadn't thought of Jamie Oliver, The Naked Chef. She was finding it difficult enough to concentrate without thinking about nakedness while stirring a bowl of melting chocolate and standing beside one of the sexiest men in Hollywood.

The delicious scent of the chocolate and warm cinnamon was intoxicating, but no more so than being in such close proximity to James. They were standing side by side at the hob, their hands occasionally touching, his leg brushing against hers. Eleanor was so hot and bothered by the time the hot chocolate was ready, she could have done with a cold shower.

James poured their drinks into fancy mugs which were copper at the bottom and glass at the top. They looked like the kind of thing you'd get in a posh cafe rather than someone's house. Then he added more glasses and a jug of iced water to the tray.

'It's very rich and thick,' he said in answer to her unspoken question. 'You might be glad of a glass of water to wash it down.'

Eleanor did think she might be glad of it.

'Let's go through to the lounge, there's a wood burner in there and we'll be nice and cosy.'

Eleanor had hoped they'd sit in the conservatory she'd spotted on the side of the house. That would have been much cooler and brighter, less suited to snuggling up close.

'I think it's important to be as comfortable as possible when you've got a confession to make, don't you?' James asked with his lazy smile.

'Confession?' Eleanor asked huskily. She thought for one awful moment he'd somehow realised what was going on inside her head.

'You're meant to be telling me what's on your mind, remember?' he prompted. 'I hope you're not going to back out now that I've made you my special hot chocolate?'

Eleanor cleared her throat. 'Oh, that,' she replied, knowing she definitely wouldn't be telling him what was on her mind at that precise moment. 'I'd almost forgotten.'

Eleanor was surprised to find that it was true and the whole first night debacle had completely slipped her mind. But now it was back with a vengeance and had much the same effect on her ardour as a bucket of cold water.

Just to be on the safe side, she deliberately opted for an armchair on one side of the fireplace rather than sitting beside James on the sofa. She poured herself a glass of the iced water and gulped it down. Then she shivered and took a sip of the deliciously rich, comforting hot chocolate.

'This is amazing!' she exclaimed, licking the thick, bittersweet liquid from her lips and taking another sip. 'I've never tasted anything quite like it. I can admit now, I wasn't too sure when you added chilli powder, I'm not keen on spicy food. But the chilli just gives it a bit of a zing. This is heavenly.'

'I told you I make a mean hot chocolate,' he said. 'So, I've held up my end of the bargain, now it's your turn.' He sat back on the sofa waiting for her to speak. When she didn't, he gently prompted. 'Has what's bothering you got anything to do with why you left home in such a hurry that you forgot to book yourself a hire car at the airport?'

Eleanor sighed. 'Yes, it has,' she admitted. She took a deep breath and started to talk, hesitantly at first. She began by telling him about some of the high and lows of directing her first play, *Heavens Above!* She mentioned Brandon Stone, then she remembered the rivalry between the two men. She reined herself in, only saying he'd struggled a bit adapting to the theatre. She felt it would be unprofessional to talk about Brandon behind his back and give James more ammunition for their famous media spats.

But James made no comment about his rival — in fact he made no comments at all. He was the ideal audience, nodding understandingly at some points, grimacing in sympathy at others.

Here, at last, was someone who really understood what she was talking about. Eleanor stopped being so guarded and gave him a blow by blow account of the opening night.

She was nearly in tears again by the time she'd finished talking. Her memories of that dreadful night were still vivid and raw. When James didn't speak, she forced herself to look up. She knew he'd be kind and say the right thing — but she wanted to try and gauge his real reaction from the look on his face before he spoke.

He looked completely stunned.

'You're joking, surely?' he demanded, jumping up from the sofa.

Eleanor was expecting him to come over and give her a big hug, but instead he rushed out of the room. She gulped. That wasn't the reaction she'd been expecting. Was he so horrified, he couldn't even bear to be in the same room?

She waited, unsure what to do, her heart thumping. The terrible thought came to her that he might refuse to carry on with the pantomime in case association with her damaged his professional reputation. Eleanor leaped to her feet and started frantically searching for her coat.

Then she heard a door. slam and heavy footsteps returning at a jog. Before she had time to flee, James burst back into the room carrying what appeared to be a huge pile of recycling.

Seriously? Eleanor felt confused, then angry. Surely he hadn't gone to get paper to add to the wood burner at a moment like this? She stood trembling, half-terrified, half-furious, waiting for the axe to fall.

'Do you never read the theatrical reviews, woman?' James demanded, throwing the recycling on the rug in front of the wood burner and getting down on his knees. 'Help me,' he commanded, pulling her down beside him and fishing out copies of The Telegraph, Time Out and The Stage. But before Eleanor had a chance to open any of them, James had found what he was looking for and started reading aloud:

'Heavens Above! What a debut! Actress Eleanor Christie has taken critics by surprise with her outstanding directorial debut. The jury was out when she chose this little-known piece by playwright Jacob Ackland-Snow and cast Hollywood bad boy Brandon Stone in the lead. But the result is nothing short of a tour de force. Watch out, West End — this show has wings!'

He grabbed more papers and started reading another extracts, while Eleanor sat on the floor in a daze. There were lots of the usual tabloid puns: 'Say Halo to hot new director, Eleanor Christie.' 'Heavens Above! This show is a gift from on high!'

Eleanor heard all the hyperbole, but the words washed over her. None of this made any sense.

'I don't understand. Brandon fell off the stage on the first night!' she blurted out.

'I know, he told me.' James grinned. 'But apparently the audience thought it was deliberate so he's having to do it every night now! The critics are hailing him as some kind of comic genius and they're crediting you with coaxing this hidden talent out of him.'

'Seriously?' Eleanor said. 'But that's insane! He was drunk, plain and simple.'.

'Of course it's insane. Showbiz is completely insane, Ella. That's why I come home regularly, to try and get my feet back on the ground again,' James explained. 'And trust me, the London theatre is fairly balanced compared with Hollywood. That really is a madhouse. But if you want my advice, you'll just go along with it like Brandon has. Acting is all about improvisation, so improvise! Act as if it was all intentional and lap up the praise while it's going. No one needs to know it was a fluke.'

Eleanor started to giggle. 'He's really got to fall off the stage every night now?' she asked.

James laughed too. 'Yeah. Poor sod! But he doesn't seem to mind. In fact, he's much happier playing the clown than he ever was trying to carry off serious roles. You've done him a massive favour, you know.'

Something started to filter through to Eleanor's confused brain. 'How do you know that?' she asked. 'I thought you and Brandon were arch enemies or something.'

'No, that's just more showbiz madness. We're good friends. But when we met a couple of years back and began spending time together the innuendoes started flying. So our agents cooked up this whole bitter rivalry and the media have lapped it up. Brandon and I get on fine. And by the way, he really is a good actor — much better than people give him credit for. He just gets nervous and makes a prat of himself sometimes.'

'I'll say,' Eleanor added drily.

'Anyway, that's enough about him. We should be talking about you and celebrating the success of *Heavens Above!* I can't believe you didn't know. Haven't your friends been phoning up and pestering you? Mine like nothing better than quoting bits out of my reviews. Especially the bad ones,' he added.

'I've lost my phone,' Eleanor explained. 'I think I left it in the theatre that night, but I couldn't face going back to look for it.'

'I'm not surprised, if you thought the play was a complete flop. And that explains why you came up here in such a hurry too. But it isn't a flop, it's a huge success!' he said, grabbing her and dancing round the room. 'Let me go and get some bubbly out of the fridge.'

Eleanor was still smiling when James came back into the room with a bottle and glasses.

'You should smile all the time, you've got a beautiful smile,' he said, unscrewing the wire top and peeling the foil off. 'I love the way it makes your eyes sparkle.'

He gave the cork an experienced twist and it shot across the room with a bang.

'Do you always keep a bottle of

champagne in the house?' she asked, trying to steer the conversation onto safer ground.

'Of course!' he replied. 'You never know when you're going to have something to celebrate. Having to put everything on hold while you go out to the supermarket kind of spoils the moment, don't you think?'

'I suppose so,' Eleanor admitted, 'though I wouldn't really know. I obviously haven't done as much celebrating as you have.'

'I'm more than happy to help you practise,' James said, handing her a glass of champagne. 'But you might find you have a lot more to celebrate if you start reading your reviews. To *Heavens Above!*' he added, raising his glass.

Eleanor touched her glass to his and smiled. '*Heavens Above!*' she repeated. She drank some champagne, which was cold and rather bitter after the hot chocolate.

'Now let's see what else they have to

say about the great Eleanor Christie,' James said, taking her hand and drawing her back down onto the rug beside him.

Eleanor laughed. She was sitting in James McIntyre's parents' front room, toasting the show she'd thought had put an end to her career. She felt dazed. The whole situation was so bizarre she wondered if she'd wake up and discover it had been a dream.

She sat on the floor surrounded by newspapers, looking at James as he leafed through for more reviews. His eyelashes were longer than she'd realised and he had a mole on his neck she'd never noticed before. Her gaze was drawn to the cleft in his chin and she imagined herself pouring a drip of chocolate into it and licking it off . . .

He must have felt her eyes on him, because he looked up.

'Are you OK, Ella?' he asked gently, putting the newspaper down.

'I'm fine, thanks. Just fine,' she

answered, blushing furiously.

'Only you seem a bit shell-shocked,' he said, reaching across to brush a strand of hair behind her ear.

His thumb caressed her hot cheek and he started to move closer as though he was about to kiss her. She was on the point of closing her eyes when he abruptly pulled away.

'Damn!' he said. 'I promised you I wouldn't. Boys' Brigade honour and all that. Remind me never to make a stupid promise like that again.'

'What if I were to release you from your promise?' Eleanor asked, reaching out and touching his chin.

'You could, if you were sure that's what you wanted,' he said slowly.

Eleanor nodded and watched his eyes light up with an inner glow.

Their lips had just touched when all hell broke loose. The dogs started barking and raced into the hall, the front door opened and there were voices in the hall.

'Did the earth move for you?' James

asked, torn between laughter and frustration.

The next thing Eleanor knew, the lounge door opened and a middle-aged couple — presumably Mr and Mrs McIntyre — walked into the room.

'Heavens above!' the woman said, taking in the scene in front of her. Then she looked to her husband for an explanation, as their son and his visitor dissolved into a heap on the floor laughing.

He shrugged. There was no accounting for young people's behaviour these days.

15

After they managed to scoop themselves off the floor, James introduced her to his parents and Eleanor spent a very pleasant evening with the family.

Joanna McIntyre whipped up an amazing stir-fry in no time at all, so Eleanor could easily see where James got his love of cooking from. James explained their hilarity over the use of the phrase 'Heavens above!' and the McIntyres insisted on opening more champagne. They seemed to keep a good supply of it in, though with a movie star for a son maybe that wasn't so surprising.

They talked easily over dinner about everything from Katie Moore and the Tullymuir panto to James's upcoming movie role, and Eleanor found herself thoroughly enjoying their company. They were as easy-going and good-natured as their son, though Ian McIntyre had such a dry sense of humour it took Eleanor a while to realise when he was joking. And after dinner, she was delighted to see that James hadn't been joking about taking out the trash. While she was helping his mother load the dishwasher, he grabbed the rubbish bag out of the kitchen bin and disappeared out of the back door with it. For a Hollywood superstar he really did have his feet on the ground.

At the end of the evening James insisted on walking Eleanor home, saying they'd all drunk too much to drive safely. But she suspected this was just an excuse to get her to himself again.

She wasn't wrong. When they were well away from his parents' house, following the road back into the village instead of taking their earlier route over the hills, he stopped and turned to her.

'Now, where were we, when we were

so rudely interrupted?'

'About here, I think,' she answered, pulling him towards her by the lapels on his heavy coat.

'Really, Miss Christie. I had no idea you were that sort of girl,' he protested, when they drew apart at last to catch their breath.

'Well if I am, it's your fault!' she retorted. 'All that melting chocolate and the scent of cinnamon and vanilla. It's enough to turn any girl's head.'

He laughed softly and his eyes sparkled. 'I know. And it works every time,' he said brazenly.

'Oh, it does, does it?' Eleanor exclaimed, pretending to be furious but letting him kiss her crossness away.

The walk home took a very long time, despite the cold, as there were frequent stops along the way for more kissing. They even paused for a final smooch in the graveyard so that Eleanor felt sure she'd never be frightened to walk past it again now that it held much happier associations.

The next morning, Janet Webster surprised and embarrassed her granddaughter by drawing attention to the state of her chin over breakfast.

'No need to ask what *you* got up to last night,' she said. 'I know a chin rubbed raw from stubble when I see one.'

'So you should,' her husband said, giving her waist a playful squeeze. 'You used to look like that all the time when we first got married.'

'Married being the appropriate word,' Janet said severely. 'Young people these days have the morals of a tom cat.'

Eleanor gasped, laughed and choked on her porridge.

'Nana, we were only kissing for heaven's sake!' she protested.

'Well, it's a short step from that to the other,' Janet warned, cryptically. She then spoiled the effect completely by giggling like a schoolgirl when Davy said, 'We could give it a go again, if you like?'

'Too much information,' Eleanor said, covering her ears and trying not to picture her grandparents canoodling.

'Well, at least he's a nice chap from a decent family. And he'd certainly be able to look after you,' Janet added.

'Nana, for the last time, we were only kissing. Can you please stop planning our wedding? I don't even know what James is really like yet. Yesterday was the first time we spent any time together when we weren't rehearsing for the panto,' she said, trying to be serious. But it was no good, Eleanor could feel the goofy grin spreading across her face, betraying her completely.

'Ah-hah,' Janet murmured. 'So when will you be seeing him again, do you think?'

'No idea,' Eleanor replied, stifling a sigh. 'I expect it'll be at the next rehearsal.'

'Really?' Davy asked, as he stood at

the sink washing up his bowl and mug. 'I think it might be a bit sooner than that, myself.'

He walked to the back door to head out to the garage as usual and left it open behind him.

'Go on in, lad, I'm sure she'll be pleased to see you,' they heard him say.

The next thing Eleanor knew, James McIntyre was standing in the kitchen. He was wearing the leather jacket she remembered from the airport and smiling as widely as she was herself.

'I just realised you haven't met Bessie yet,' he said, after wishing them both a good morning.

'Who's Bessie?'

'Come with me and I'll show you,' he said, holding out his hand. 'You might want to put something on, it's cold out there.'

Eleanor grabbed her jacket and put her hand in his. She tried not to be distracted by the tingle that ran like an electric shock from her fingers up her arm and through her whole body. She felt her heart beat faster and followed James outside, still holding his hand. When they were out of sight of the kitchen window, he pulled her towards him and kissed her again. Eleanor never wanted it to stop, but the sound of her grandfather very purposefully clearing his throat on the way past brought them back to reality.

'Ah yes,' James said. 'Bessie.'

He led her to the front of the house where there were a few cars parked on the road. Eleanor didn't know whether Bessie was a person or an animal but it looked as though they were going to have to drive somewhere to meet her. So she was a bit surprised when James stopped beside a large black and silver motorbike.

'This is Bessie,' he said proudly.

Eleanor stared at the bike and then at James, who held out a spare motorbike helmet for her to put on.

'Ah, that explains your comment at the airport about luggage,' Eleanor said, stalling for time. 'Are you sure you want to go for a ride, right now?' she asked. 'You've only just got here.'

'There's nothing to be scared of,' James said, correctly interpreting her reluctance. 'You'll be perfectly safe with me.'

And Eleanor realised that she did feel safe with James, that she trusted him completely. So even though she'd never been on a motorbike before and was terrified at the idea, she held out a hand — which was shaking only slightly — and took the helmet. As she put it on, she felt like an astronaut or a diver setting off on an adventure.

'Your carriage awaits,' James said with a flourish and a bow. He then spoiled the effect somewhat by adding, 'Hop on.'

Eleanor clambered on behind him and wrapped her arms around him. The next thing she knew, they were driving sedately through the village. It was only when they reached the last house that James opened up the throttle a little and they picked up speed. Eleanor felt as though she was flying, even though she suspected he was driving much more slowly than usual for her benefit. Having her arms wrapped tightly round him was bliss, even though if wasn't strictly necessary. And disappointingly, she couldn't really feel his body through the thick leather of his jacket. She was just starting to relax and enjoy herself when James's voice spoke in her ear, making her jump.

'How are you doing?' he asked.

'Fine,' she replied. 'But how are you doing that? I shouldn't be able to hear you, should I?'

James lifted his left hand and pointed to a black lump of plastic on the side of the helmet.

'It's a bluetooth communicator. Means we can talk while we ride, or listen to music or whatever. It's great for long journeys. So what do you think?'

'It's very clever. I didn't know you could get things like that,' she replied.

She heard his soft chuckle in her ear.

'Not the bluetooth, silly! I meant the whole bike-riding experience.'

'Well, I'm enjoying it so far,' she admitted. 'Only I was wondering if we could go a little faster?'

'You got it!' James gave a yawp of delight.

And then Eleanor really got to feel the power of the machine. She'd travelled these roads a thousand times, but it felt completely different being on the back of a motorbike instead of enclosed inside a car. She was very aware of the black surface of the road beneath their wheels and could feel the cold air on the exposed parts of her skin. With no window separating her from the world she felt more part of the landscape, as though she could reach out and touch the leaves on the trees and hedges as they whizzed past.

By the time James pulled over at a viewing point beside a loch, she was completely enthralled by the whole experience.

'It's so exhilarating!' she enthused,

watching James's smile broaden. 'The only thing I don't get is why you would call a beast of a machine like this Bessie? It's not even vaguely appropriate.'

James laughed. 'That's the whole point. You see Mum's never come round to the idea of me riding motorbikes, even though I've been doing it for years now. So I always make a point of giving my bikes names like Bessie or Maud, which sound warm and friendly and most of all, safe! She's much happier when I say I'm going off to ride Bessie, than she would be if I told her I was going out on my motorbike.'

Eleanor smiled. 'That makes perfect sense.'

* * *

Being with James made perfect sense, too, and from then on they started spending a lot of time together. When they weren't discussing the panto and using their combined talents to raise it from a little local production into something truly memorable, they were going for walks in the hills or rides on Bessie, sitting in quiet pubs by roaring fires chatting for hours, or going out for dinner and a movie.

Best of all, Eleanor loved spending time at James's parents' house where she was always welcomed with open arms. She spent many a happy afternoon there helping James learn lines for his upcoming movie role and discussing ideas for her own next project. Now that the spectre of *Heavens Above!* wasn't looming over her, Eleanor felt she could breathe again and ideas started coming thick and fast.

So they talked about their work and themselves and started to get to know and like each other more every day. Neither mentioned the fact that come January, their idyll would be over, James would go back to LA and the bubble would burst.

One day they were sitting having

coffee in the cosy little nook of a tiny pub. It was by one of the lesser-known lochs and 'was a perfect gem of a place. Because James liked to keep out of the public eye when he was at home, he knew all the best hideaways and he was introducing Eleanor to his favourites.

She visited places she'd never been to in her life, many of them only just up the road from Tullymuir. They walked the whole way round the loch holding hands, stopping for the occasional smooch and chatting all the time.

It was a bright, chilly day and the sky with its scudding clouds was reflected perfectly in the dark waters of the loch. When James got Eleanor to bend sideways and twist her head round so she could see the reflection of the pub the right way up in the water, she felt herself fall in love with him a little bit more. James seemed to have the ability to see the world in a different way and when Eleanor was with him she felt her eyes being opened to new possibilities.

Eventually they retreated from the

cold into the cosy little pub to rest and warm up. When James took off his coat to throw it over the back of a chair he noticed the stiff cardboard envelope sticking out of his pocket.

'Ah yes, I meant to give you this,' he said, handing it to Eleanor.

'What is it?'

'Open it and see,' he replied, smiling.

Eleanor's cold fingers fumbled with the stiff envelope and pulled out a thick cream piece of card with gold edges. It looked like a posh wedding invitation, but the curly writing on it told her it was an invitation to a Ball.

'I thought we should get some practice in by going to a real ball before we have to act it out in the panto,' James explained, smiling.

'I didn't know you were into method acting!'

'You mean like having myself locked in a cell, if I'm playing the part of a prisoner? No, I'm not into that at all, I'd far rather just learn my lines, turn up on the day and act. The invitation to the Hunt Ball has nothing to do with the panto at all,' he admitted, 'it's really just an excuse to get you to go out with me again.'

'You don't need an excuse,' Eleanor replied, her eyes sparkling. Then her face fell. 'But did you say Hunt Ball? I thought those were only for people who . . . well . . . hunted, I suppose. And I really don't approve of hunting. Shouldn't this just be for the Lord of the Manor and his cronies? How come you've even been invited to this?'

'I guess it would have been like that in the old days when it actually was a hunt ball, but now it's the Muirfield Ball and is basically just a big party. Anyone can buy a ticket. You're more likely to meet a local businessman there than a huntsman these days. And it attracts all kinds of people from the arts, like writers, actors and television celebrities. I even met a film director there once.'

'I thought you didn't like going to parties?' Eleanor teased.

'I don't, that's why I'm asking you to come with me. If I'm spending the evening with you, at least I know I'll have a good time.'

'Charmer!' she retorted. 'But why do you have to go at all?'

'I don't have to go, but it's a bit of a family tradition. Dad helped Lord Ferguson out with a legal problem years ago and since then, he's put a lot of estate business Dad's way. So Mum and Dad always get invited — a proper invitation, not a bought one. I started going along when I was old enough, first as a waiter — you know, the guys circulating with trays of drinks?' Eleanor nodded. 'Well, I was one of those,' James continued. 'I actually made some good contacts there when I was starting out in the business. Now Dad likes me to go along. He thinks I'll act as a bit of a draw, to be honest,' he admitted, looking embarrassed. 'People like to know there'll be a few famous faces there. And the more guests, the more money gets raised at the big charity auction held after dinner.'

'Ah, I see. So it's a kind of a duty thing but all for a good cause.'

'I suppose you could put it that way. But it's quite an experience too. It's not just another party. For starters it's white tie, so the men are all in tails or dinner jackets and kilts and the women wear ball gowns.'

'Kilts, you say?' Eleanor asked, smirking.

'Well, you can count me in then.'

'Really?' James asked, bemused.

'Mmm, hmmm! I can't wait to see you in a kilt,' Eleanor said rather huskily.

'You just want to find out if what they say is true,' James teased.

'What's that, then?' Eleanor asked, trying to banish the image of James in a kilt from her mind.

'Whether Scotsmen wear anything under their kilts or not,' he answered.

'No I don't,' Eleanor denied hotly, blushing a fiery red and taking a gulp of coffee that made her choke.

James wouldn't stop teasing her about it all afternoon.

* * *

With the two leads madly in love, the rehearsals for Cinderella really started to come along apace. The atmosphere fizzed with the chemistry between them and their performances sparkled, encouraging the rest of the cast to raise their game. The Fairy Godmother became sweeter and kinder, the Wicked Stepmother more cruel and frightening by contrast and Tommy and Hamish nearly stole the show as the riotous Ugly Sisters.

Just seeing the two men with their large frames and weather-roughened skin dressed in corsets and petticoats was enough to make anyone laugh. They rolled around the stage in their high heels for all the world like sailors on the swaying deck of a ship. And they made no attempt to disguise their voices, so that their lines were delivered in deep baritones. The hall rang to the sound of laughter and the cast carried their joy and enthusiasm to The Old Thistle after each rehearsal, so that everyone in the pub was desperate to see the show. News spread and soon there wasn't a ticket left.

★ ★ ★

One evening when the cast had retired to the pub for a post-rehearsal discussion, talk turned to the Hunt Ball. Eleanor discovered that James had been right, it was open to anyone and quite a few of the cast would be there. They were all very much looking forward to it.

'It's a great excuse to get dressed up,' Betty McCardle declared. 'It's not often you get the chance wear a ball gown. And the men look gorgeous in their DJs and kilts,' she added, fluttering her eyelashes at James. 'Not that I'll be wearing anything particularly glam — ' she gestured towards her enormous bump — 'at this rate the only thing that'll fit me is a tent!'

Everyone laughed. Even in a tent Betty would look good. Pregnancy was suiting her and she had a real bloom in her cheeks and a sparkle in her eyes.

And it certainly wasn't stopping her flirting. She was always smiling at James and trying to catch his eye or 'accidentally' brushing against him. Eleanor would have been cross if it hadn't been so funny to watch.

She nudged Fiona, who smiled at Betty's antics.

'Will you come shopping with me for a dress?' Eleanor asked her. 'I don't have anything remotely suitable here to wear.'

'Of course. I'll need to get something new myself — I can't drag out the same old dress I've worn for the last two years.'

'You're going, too?' Eleanor asked.

'Of course. The doctors take a table at the Muirfield Ball for our Christmas do every year. We've got a bit of a competition going with the local vets to see whose table is the rowdiest. Actually, I'm going with Andrew this year,' Fiona added, nonchalantly, though a fiery blush suffused her cheeks.

'Ah, I meant to ask how you and the delectable Dr McFarlaine had been getting on,' Eleanor teased. 'Obviously very well.'

'You can talk!' Fiona retorted. 'You and James seem to be joined at the hip these days.'

They both grinned, their eyes alight with joy.

'Happy?' Eleanor asked, undercover of the general noise and hubbub.

'Very,' Fiona replied and her broad grin and sparkling eyes confirmed it. 'Me too.'

'I can see that,' Fiona said. 'You've almost got as much of a glow about you as Betty has. Do you love him?'

'Yes,' Eleanor replied, without hesitation.

'Only . . . ' Fiona paused.

'Only what?'

'Well, I don't mean to be a party

pooper, and you've probably already got it all worked out anyway, but what happens when James goes back to the States?'

Eleanor wriggled uncomfortably. Fiona had always asked hard questions. And if anything, she was even more direct these days.

It was probably her nursing background, Eleanor reflected. It meant she didn't beat about the bush or come out with all the usual platitudes, she tackled thorny issues head on.

'I don't know,' Eleanor admitted, taking a gulp of her red wine. 'I'm trying not to think about any of that.'

'That's not going to help, though, is it?' Fiona pointed out. 'And what does James have to say about it?'

'We haven't exactly discussed it,' Eleanor confessed.

'Well, don't you think it's about time you did?'

16

Eleanor knew her friend was right. But she didn't even want to think about what was going to happen when the pantomime was over — never mind broach the subject with James.

For the moment, they were living in a fairytale that Eleanor simply never wanted to end. Fiona didn't seem to realise how lucky she and Andrew were. They lived in the same world; sometimes they even worked in the same hospital. If their relationship prospered, Eleanor could imagine them living in the Highlands for the rest of their lives, in a large, messy house filled with noisy children.

She and James did have acting in common, but their worlds were miles apart. She worked in the theatre, which didn't pay well and was likely to mean spending long periods of time either in

London or one of the other big cities.

James probably got paid a fortune for his movie roles and travelled all round the world. She knew the science fiction blockbuster he'd recently been in was filmed somewhere in North Africa, because he'd told her a little about it.

She lived in a quirky little flat above a dry cleaners in Bloomsbury, where she had to climb a glorified ladder to reach her bedroom. James, on the other hand, had a house with a pool somewhere in LA.

No, she decided, it was best not to think about it. While she ignored the issue, she and James could carry on living in their bubble, untouched by reality.

★ ★ ★

James was worried. This unplanned and un-looked-for relationship with Eleanor was developing at quite a pace. But that wasn't what was bothering him. He already knew exactly how he felt about her — he'd known from the start and he had a very clear picture in his head of where he would like it to go. But there were two problems starting to loom large on the horizon.

The first was Brandon Stone. James still hadn't admitted to his friend that he knew exactly where Brandon's missing director was. He felt a bit bad about that, since his friend seemed so keen to find her. But why? Why was he searching everywhere for Eleanor? Did Brandon want to find her so he could apologise for his appalling behaviour on the opening night of *Heavens Above?* Did he want to thank her for discovering his hidden comedic talent? Or was he trying so desperately to track her down because he'd lost his heart to her too?

That last thought was giving James sleepless nights. Even though Brandon had told him countless times how he didn't feel as though he fitted in with the whole Hollywood scene, he certainly looked the part of a movie star.

He was the archetypal tall, dark and handsome hero. James felt like a very poor second, by comparison.

He wasn't being guilty of false modesty; he knew that his particular look seemed to be in at the moment and girls had always found him attractive. But he could never quite work out why. When he looked in the mirror he just saw the same old face looking back at him. So he really didn't want Brandon turning up, trying to sweep Eleanor off her feet.

The other thing troubling him was knowing that Katie Jayne Mitchell was trying to track him down. She'd already sent him several text messages, which he'd immediately deleted. How on earth had she managed to get his phone number?

Now that really was a worry. It was another reason he'd been so keen to get away from Hollywood. Katie Jayne was rumoured to be his leading lady in the next movie he was making, though she was actually only one of the three actresses auditioning for the part. But she had quite a reputation. Eleanor had teased him the other day about method acting, but from what he'd heard, that was Katie Jayne's approach exactly. Or rather, whenever a part called on her to fall in love with her leading man on screen she'd track down the poor sod who was going to be playing opposite her and make a play for him.

She'd ruined several relationships that James knew of and had split up one long-term marriage. She didn't seem to care how many lives she wrecked, she would do whatever it took to make a movie work. He'd felt much safer being five thousand miles away from her with an ocean in between. But getting those text messages had unsettled him. He wouldn't put it past her to come after him — and, from what he'd heard, when Katie Jayne Mitchell had you in her sights there was no escape.

James tried to put all his concerns to the back of his mind and concentrate

on Eleanor and the here and now
— both of which were pretty amazing.
He'd never met anyone quite like
Eleanor Christie before. She was
absolutely gorgeous, he'd spotted that
right away at the airport. But James was
coming to realise that she was just as
nice on the inside as she looked on the
outside.

She'd given Brandon his big break
into theatre, even though his nerves and
drunkenness had made him a nightmare to work with. She'd come to visit
her grandparents for a break and had
ended up directing and starring in the
local panto to help them, the local
community and her old drama teacher.
She was kind and funny and down to
earth.

She was also touchingly vulnerable.
The fact that she'd run away after the
opening night of *Heavens Above!* and
had been too terrified to read the
reviews was rather endearing.

She didn't seem to have developed
the thick skin needed to survive in the

industry at all. Most actresses looked as though a stiff gust of wind would blow them over, but in reality they were tough as old boots and they'd sell their grannies to advance their careers.

Eleanor wasn't like that at all. When he was with her, James felt as though he could quite happily give up Hollywood, the fame and riches — despite all the hard work it had taken to get there — to be with her.

But he didn't think such dramatic measures were necessary. They were both actors, both good at what they did and respected in their fields. He could probably find work in the UK either in homegrown films, which was where he'd started out anyway, on television or in the theatre.

And he had no doubt Eleanor would go down a storm in Hollywood if she wanted to give it a go. He knew there was nothing they couldn't do if they put their minds and talents together. No, James had high hopes of his future with Eleanor . . . if only Brandon Stone and

Katie Jayne Mitchell would keep out of the way.

*　*　*

Eleanor and Fiona were struggling to find a day to go shopping for dresses for the Muirfield Ball. Even though Eleanor often had evening events to go to, she'd never been a keen shopper and was happiest in jeans. But at least when she was in London, if she had to dress up for an occasion, she knew exactly where to go and could usually find something suitable in a couple of hours.

Up here, she had no idea where to start. Fiona told her to leave it up to her to arrange their ballgown-buying expedition, which was a relief. But it was getting worryingly close to the day of the ball by the time Fiona managed to sort out a day off and she had to do a fair bit of shift swapping to manage it.

'Right, I've got Friday off, so we can go shopping for our ballgowns then,' Fiona said when she phoned to tell

Eleanor the news. 'Sorry to cut it so fine.'

'We've got ages yet,' Eleanor said. 'The Ball's not until next weekend.'

'Next weekend is the panto, silly. The Muirfield Ball is on Wednesday night.'

'Who on earth holds a massive party on a Wednesday night?' she asked, scrabbling through her bag for the invitation and discovering her friend was quite right.

'It's always been on a Wednesday. I've no idea why. It probably dates back to the days when it was only the local gentry who went — they wouldn't have had to worry about getting up for work the next day. Most people just book the next day off to recover.'

'Seems daft to me,' Eleanor grumbled.

'I don't know what you're complaining about, you're not even working at the moment. And no, directing the local panto doesn't count as real work!'

'It's actually pretty hard going a lot of the time,' Eleanor argued.

'It might have been to start with, but

now it's just an excuse for you to spend time with James.'

They decided to make the most of their shopping day, setting out early on the Friday morning and popping in to the corner shop for takeaway coffee and croissants on the way. Eleanor had been surprised to find out the McBride sisters' shop ran to such luxuries.

'We're not as backward here in Tullymuir as you seem to think,' Fiona said irritably — which reminded Eleanor that her friend was never at her best first thing in the morning, at least not until she'd had several cups of coffee.

'Aggie and Bridie are always keen to find new ways to make money,' Fiona explained, as she pulled up outside. 'They started by doing hot sausage rolls and sandwiches for lunches when they realised a lot of people stopped by to pick up a newspaper on their way to work. Then they moved on to croissants, Danish pastries and hot drinks. Now they do a roaring trade in both breakfast and lunches. Those two never miss a trick.'

'Not working today, Fiona?' Aggie demanded, before their feet had crossed the threshold.

She was sorting through piles of newspapers, but stopped what she was doing to interrogate them. If it hadn't been for the delicious smell of baking and the promise of coffee, Eleanor would have been tempted to turn tail and run. But Fiona was made of sterner stuff — or perhaps she was just inured to the sisters' nosiness.

'No,' she replied shortly.

'Only you're not wearing your uniform,' Aggie pointed out.

'That's right,' Fiona said.

'You're up and about early today, Eleanor,' Bridie joined in, appearing from somewhere out the back with a wicker tray of warm croissants.

'Things to do, you know,' Eleanor said, trying to copy Fiona's tactics and be vague.

'Oh aye. What things would those

be?' Bridie demanded, keeping a firm hold on the tray of croissants.

'We need dresses for the Hunt Ball,' Fiona said.

Eleanor glared at her. 'Why on earth did you tell them that?' she muttered out of the corner of her mouth.

'We'll never get our breakfast if we don't give them some information,' Fiona whispered back.

Aggie spent the next five minutes advising them on the best shops to try in Inverness, and she and Bridie got into a brief but heated argument about whether Highland House of Fraser or Chisholm's Highland Dress was the better outfitter.

'You'll be going with young Jimmy McIntyre, I suppose?' Aggie said, looking pointedly at Eleanor.

There was no point in denying it. Besides, Bridie was putting the lids on the takeaway coffees at a rate that would put a sloth to shame, obviously waiting for Eleanor's answer.

'Yes, I am,' Eleanor replied, hoping to

move things along by agreeing. But she couldn't stop herself smiling at the thought of James.

'Hmm, we'll have to wait and see now, won't we?' Aggie said cryptically.

'What do you mean?' Eleanor asked, before she could stop herself.

'It's just that with that American actress turning up, we wondered if he might be taking her,' Bridie asked, watching closely for Eleanor's reaction.

Eleanor looked at her blankly.

'We've no idea what you're talking about,' Fiona snapped, impatient to leave and clearly desperate for her coffee.

'Must be a coincidence then, her arriving just before the ball,' Aggie observed. She made it sound like the least likely coincidence she'd ever heard of.

'Must be,' Fiona said firmly.

While she and Eleanor paid, gathered their purchases and left, Bridie had time for one more barb.

'We're not saying she's his girlfriend

250

or anything like that. I'm sure James would never go out with two girls at the same time. But I've definitely seen their names coupled together in those celebrity magazines.'

Eleanor left the shop feeling exhausted. Encounters with the McBride sisters tended to have that effect on people. It was a shame theirs was the only grocery shop in the village; the fact that it was the Post Office as well meant they had the locals at their mercy.

Unless people had a car and were prepared to drive as far as Inverbruin, they had no choice but to brave the lion's den.

'What do you think that was all about?' Eleanor asked her friend as they finally set off.

'No idea,' Fiona replied. 'But I really wouldn't worry about it. You know what those two are like, they're always out to make trouble.'

'I know that, but I can't help wondering who the American actress is. And what she's doing in Tullymuir.'

'If she's even here at all,' Fiona pointed out. 'They didn't say which actress they were talking about. Maybe one of them spotted someone who looked a bit like a famous actress and they're just making mischief for the sake of it. I wouldn't put it past them.' She turned to smile at Eleanor. 'And I don't think you've got anything to worry about anyway. I saw the way James looked at you in the pub the other night. That man has fallen for you hook, line and sinker!'

Eleanor grinned. She knew her friend was probably right and although she hadn't known James very long, she trusted him implicitly. But it did seem more than a little odd that sleepy old Tullymuir was suddenly becoming a magnet for the rich and famous.

As they wandered round Inverness trying to find suitable dresses, the thought kept niggling at the back of her mind: who was the American actress and what was she doing in Tullymuir two days before the Muirfield Ball?

17

On the day of the ball, Eleanor's grandfather took her out to his workshop to show her what he'd been working on.

She'd asked several times about his latest project, which had been keeping him out in the garage even more than usual, but he'd refused point blank to tell her. She'd been wondering what the mystery was, but knew he'd explain in his own good time.

And the time finally seemed to have arrived. When her grandfather turned the light on, Eleanor spotted James and her grandmother standing in the corner. She just had time to notice that James wasn't looking his usual self when they both shouted, 'Surprise!' James had a bottle of champagne in his hand and her nana was holding a tray with four glasses on it. In the middle of the garage, covered with an old dustsheet, was the rounded shape of a car.

'What on earth's going on?' she asked, looking at them all in confusion.

'Tell her, Davy,' James prompted.

But instead of saying anything, Davy Webster reached for a corner of the dust sheet and twitched it off. They all blinked. There in front of them was a VW Beetle, which looked as though it had just been driven out of a car showroom. It had pristine, pearlescent white paintwork that shimmered and sparkled under the electric lights.

'That's beautiful!' Eleanor exclaimed. 'It looks as though it's covered in mother-of-pearl. This isn't that old orange car that sat on the drive for years, is it? I noticed you'd covered it with tarpaulin on the night I arrived. And then it disappeared.'

'Oh, you spotted that, did you?' her grandfather asked. 'Well, it's no longer a pumpkin — now it's a car fit to take Cinderella to the ball.'

'Can I really drive it to the ball tonight?' Eleanor asked. 'Oooh, James, I can come and pick you up for a change. What do you think?'

He smiled, though it looked little forced.

'Very modern — Cinders driving Prince Charming to the ball. I like it! You won't be able to drive home though, unless you're planning on not drinking. But a lot of people leave their cars at the manor, get a taxi home, then pick them up the next day.'

'Would it be OK for me to leave it at the manor overnight?' Eleanor asked.

'Of course,' her grandfather replied. 'It's your car — you can do whatever you like with it.'

'It's really mine ... to keep?' she asked, dumbfounded, turning to her grandfather.

'Yes.' He grinned. 'Do you like it?'

She went over and gave him the biggest hug.

'It's absolutely gorgeous! But I don't understand what it's for,' she added.

'Er — driving,' James suggested. 'That's what you usually do with a car.'

'Ha ha,' Eleanor said, rolling her eyes at him. 'I get that. I just don't understand why you're giving it to me,' she added, turning back to her grandfather.

'Your grandfather and I wanted to say thank you for helping save the panto,' Janet butted in, 'and we thought it would be useful for you to have a way of getting around while you're staying here. You can't always be getting lifts from Fiona or going round on that motorbike of his,' she added, giving James a disapproving look.

Eleanor knew it was only the bike her grandmother disapproved of, not James himself.

'Nana is being kind and covering for me, but there's more to it than that,' Davy admitted. 'The truth is, when your mum was young and had just passed her driving test, I promised I'd do up a Beetle for her sometime. She wanted one in daffodil yellow. But I was still working at the time and never got round to it. I've always felt guilty about that. So I thought, better late than never. I didn't manage it for my own daughter, so I've done it for hers instead.'

Eleanor gave her grandfather another hug.

'You've got nothing to feel guilty about, Grandpa. Mum is always saying what a wonderful father you are and what an amazing childhood the two of you gave her. And I know what she means. You've both always been so good to me. I feel as though Tullymuir is my second home. Thank you,' she said, going over and giving her grandmother a hug too.

Eleanor wiped a stray tear from her eye and Janet blew her nose into the plain white handkerchief she always carried.

'Nonsense, you know you're always welcome here,' Janet said, a little gruffly.

'Hey, come on, you two,' James

257

chided them, 'this is supposed to be a celebration!'

'James is right. That's enough of that. Get that bottle opened, son — that'll give them something else to think about.'

'Yes, sir,' James said, popping the cork and pouring everyone a drink.

'To Ella and James,' Davy said. They all turned to look at him in varying degrees of surprise. It sounded like the kind of toast people made to the bride and groom at a wedding. 'I mean, for saving the panto,' he added hastily.

'And the Tullymuir Dramatic Society,' Janet added.

'To saving Cinderella,' James said smoothly and they all clinked their glasses and drank.

★ ★ ★

Eleanor didn't get a chance to talk to James in private before he had to dash away. She'd wanted to ask him if everything was OK. He looked tired and strained, not at all like someone getting ready for what promised to be an amazing night out. Fiona had told her what she could expect at her first Hunt Ball and Eleanor was really looking forward to it.

'It's very traditional,' Fiona had said when they stopped for lunch during their dress-buying expedition. 'Not like the ones where they hire a marquee and everyone sits and eats their dinner in the middle of a field. There's a proper sit-down meal in the main hall, followed by the charity auction. Then the actual ball, the dancing bit, begins around ten-ish. There's traditional Scottish dancing — reels and all that — in the ballroom. Then a break for a light supper before the music kicks off again and the dancing goes on for the rest of the night. The whole thing is rounded off with breakfast at first light for whoever's still standing by then.'

'I don't imagine there are many,' Eleanor commented.

'You'd be surprised,' Fiona said. 'Some of the older people are tough as old boots and keep going all night. It's the younger ones who tend to flag, mainly because they get carried away and overdo the alcohol too early instead of pacing themselves.'

'Spoken like a seasoned professional,' Eleanor teased. 'Is it Scottish music and dancing all night, then?'

'Not at all,' Fiona assured her. 'A few years back when Lord Ferguson noticed there weren't as many young people attending he decided to branch out a bit. Now there's a marquee outside with local bands and a DJ. Last time there was even a casino and we were all given some funny money to gamble with. It was great fun.'

Eleanor was loving the sound of the whole thing. But it was still the thought of James in a kilt that really got her pulse racing.

★ ★ ★

The girls had agreed to get ready for the ball together. So in the afternoon

Eleanor drove over to Fiona's house. She took her outfit, make-up, nail varnish and a choice of several gauzy scarves — courtesy of Janet — for them both to try on.

Fiona was in charge of hair, so had promised to have brushes for curling or straighteners depending on what styles they each opted for. When Eleanor arrived, Fiona had already begun the difficult task of taming her wild, blonde curls.

'Ooh, you look really glam already!' Eleanor said, when her friend opened the front door.

'Do you think it suits me?' Fiona asked, anxiously. 'I feel a bit lost without my curls, to be honest.'

'You look very chic and sophisticated,' Eleanor reassured her. 'Your curls are great for everyday but for a special night out, I think the smooth look is perfect for you.'

Fiona breathed a sigh of relief. Then she spotted the white car glistening in the afternoon sunshine and pushed past her friend for a closer look.

'Whose car have you borrowed?' she asked, wandering outside in her dressing gown. 'It's gorgeous!'

'It's mine,' Eleanor said proudly. 'Grandpa gave it to me this morning. He's been working on it ever since I got here and I'm going to drive James to the ball in it tonight.'

'Now that's what I call stylish. What a shame Andrew's booked us a taxi, I'd love to arrive at the ball in a car like this. It's the next best thing to going in a carriage.'

'You're welcome to cancel the taxi and join us,' Eleanor offered.

'I'm sorely tempted,' Fiona said, looking enviously at the shiny VW Beetle.

After admiring the car inside out — from its comfy leather seats and wooden dashboard to its pristine paintwork and shiny hub caps — the two friends decided to start on their own transformation.

'I can't believe it's the same old car

that sat on the drive all those years. Do you remember that time we made it into a giant pumpkin for Hallowe'en?' Eleanor asked.

'How could I possibly forget? It's just as well your nana came out and stopped us putting candles inside like we'd planned. We'd probably have burned the whole place down! But we don't have time for a trip down memory lane — we need to transform ourselves from pumpkins into princesses!' Fiona said decisively.

'Hey, less of the pumpkin, thanks! I know I've put on a few pounds since coming to Tullymuir but I'm hardly pumpkin-shaped . . . yet.'

The two friends giggled and headed excitedly into Fiona's house to begin beautifying themselves.

Eleanor started by hanging up the suit carrier with her precious outfit inside. She unzipped it and took a sneaky peek. She caught a flash of kingfisher blue and the glitter of sequins before she hurriedly zipped it up again.

She couldn't quite believe she'd managed to find such a wonderful outfit, but with Fiona's help it hadn't been too difficult. On their shopping expedition in Inverness, Fiona had taken them straight to a shop selling traditional Highland evening dress and had quickly found a black dress with a tartan over-the-shoulder sash for herself. But Eleanor had refused point-blank to wear one.

'I know Tullymuir is my second home,' she'd protested, 'but I'm not Scottish and I'd feel a complete fraud decking myself out in a tartan I'm not entitled to wear.'

'I shouldn't worry about that,' Fiona had said. 'No one else does.'

But Eleanor was adamant, and Fiona had humoured her. They'd trudged around for ages, getting nowhere until they stumbled across a quirky vintage clothes emporium which Fiona swore hadn't been there the last time she'd come shopping in Inverness.

On the very first rail of clothes

Eleanor spotted when she walked through the door was the outfit of her dreams. It was in her favourite king-fisher blue, which was what drew her to it right away. The skirt reached down to her ankles, and the matching sleeveless top had inch-wide ribbon shoulder straps. The underskirt and camisole-style top were made of a silky fabric, which felt wonderful against her skin when she tried it on. But what made it really unusual was the layer of netting covering both the skirt and top. It had a tracery of leaves and flowers embroidered on it in the same shade of blue, so that it was only noticeable up close, and was inlaid with tiny sparkly sequins that caught the light.

When Eleanor tried it on, she felt like a princess and knew it would be the perfect outfit for a ball. She couldn't wait to see James's reaction when he saw her wearing it.

But she was in for a disappointment. She'd just finished curling her hair into long, sleek waves like a 1940s film star when Fiona's mobile rang.

Fiona's face fell as she listened to what the caller was saying.

'Right, I'll tell her, Janet, thanks for ringing.'

'What's the matter? Is something wrong?'

'Not exactly. It's just that James called and left a message with your grandparents telling you not to pick him up. Apparently something's come up that he's got to deal with before he can go to the ball. He said just to go ahead and he'll meet you there.'

'Oh,' Eleanor said, unable to keep the disappointment out of her voice. 'I wonder what's happened? He knew how much I was looking forward to driving us to the ball in my new car, so whatever it is must be fairly important. I hope it's nothing too serious.'

'It can't be all that serious if he's still able to go to the ball,' Fiona replied. 'But I'm sure it's nothing to worry about.'

'You're right. He's probably just tied

up with his agent or something.'

'Probably,' Fiona agreed.

She didn't say anything else, but Eleanor knew her friend well enough to guess what she was thinking. At this moment she was probably silently cursing James and praying he wasn't about to turn from a handsome prince into a frog. That tended to be the way round it worked in real life, despite what the fairytales said.

Until that moment Eleanor had completely forgotten the McBride sisters' comments about the American actress, but now they came back to her and she found herself wondering if they'd been right after all.

'How about you drive me and Andrew instead?' Fiona said, after an awkward silence. 'You know I've had my eyes on that car of yours since you arrived!'

Eleanor gave her friend a big hug, which threatened to undo all the effort they'd put into their hair and make-up. Whatever happened tonight, she knew she could rely on Fiona.

18

Eleanor drove to Andrew McFarlaine's house to collect him, with Fiona giving directions. He'd obviously been watching out for them, as he appeared outside as soon as they pulled up.

Flona raised her eyebrows when she saw him and as he turned away to lock his front door, she gave a low murmur of appreciation.

'Mmm, hmmm,' she said. 'There's nothing quite like a man in a kilt.'

'I couldn't agree more,' Eleanor said, grinning. If even the quiet doctor could look that good in a kilt, she couldn't wait to see James in his.

Fiona leaped out of the car to say hello to Andrew and to give him a quick kiss. But it turned into a more lingering one as he shyly handed her a corsage to wear on her dress.

Eleanor quickly looked away. When

Fiona hopped into the back seat with Andrew beside her, she was rosy-cheeked and looked happier than Eleanor had ever seen her. Her friend's eyes sparkled, she looked ten years younger and there was no sign of her usual tiredness. She had no doubt at all that her friend had found her happy ending.

Eleanor smiled to herself and joined in with the excited chatter from the back seat as she drove. She tried not to eavesdrop when their voices dropped lower, but she couldn't help overhearing some of the couple's conversation. It was just everyday talk about their work and families, but there was a closeness and familiarity that made them sound as though they'd been together much longer than a matter of weeks.

It didn't take much of a leap of the imagination to picture them, years from now, an old happily married couple. Eleanor felt a warm fuzzy glow inside and tried to focus on her friend's happiness, rather than her own, more uncertain relationship with James.

★ ★ ★

When Eleanor turned off the road, through the wrought iron gates, onto the long, straight drive leading up to the big house, she and Fiona both gasped. Lanterns had been set on either side of the drive to light the way, and floodlights made the building in the distance appear to float out of the darkness. The whole effect was magical and Eleanor had to force herself to concentrate hard to avoid the large potholes in the drive.

Although she'd driven past the place countless times, all she'd ever seen was an expanse of parkland with the occasional deer roaming about. The long drive and all the surrounding mature trees made the house virtually invisible from the road. The most she'd ever managed was a brief glimpse of slate roof, one time in the depths of winter, when some of the trees had lost their leaves.

Now she could see that the house was a solid-looking grey building, with tall mullioned windows and a circular tower in one corner. It looked so much like something out of the Harry Potter movies that Eleanor expected to see people in cloaks and pointed hats. She smiled to herself at the thought. But when she got closer to the house, she could see that all the guests were appropriately attired in evening wear — not a pointed hat in sight — and only one rather elderly lady wearing a heavy woollen cloak.

Eleanor had to stop the car completely at the top of the drive while people climbed out of the cars and taxis in front of them. She noticed several people giving her new car admiring glances, which made her feel a bit more confident.

She was forced to drive at a snail's pace to avoid all the people milling around as a queue formed at the main entrance. At least this gave her a chance to admire the fountain, which threw jets of water up into the air that caught the light and sparkled like golden fireworks.

She dragged her eyes away from it and followed hand-written signs pointing to the left of the house, where a paved area had been turned into a car park for the night.

Eleanor would have felt less nervous if she'd had James at her side. It was a bit awkward turning up to such a grand affair without a partner and she was very glad of Fiona and Andrew's company. She couldn't help wondering where James was, what he was doing and when he was going to turn up. It was a bit much to invite her to this posh do and then abandon her! The McBride sisters' comments about the American actress kept popping into her head as well, which really wasn't helping.

She sighed. She wished she felt as happy and carefree as Fiona, who seemed to be floating on cloud nine. She didn't begrudge her friend her good fortune, just wished that a little of it could rub off on to her.

She marvelled at the fact that Fiona was also completely unfazed by their magnificent surroundings, which were making Eleanor feel distinctly uncomfortable. But then, she reminded herself, Fiona was on the arm of the man she loved and attended the ball each year with her work colleagues, while Eleanor was alone and had never set foot in a place like this before in her life.

The only advantage she had was her years of acting experience and she decided to call on that now, imagining the house to be a giant stage set.

As she climbed out of the car, Eleanor pretended she was playing the part of a wealthy heiress visiting friends at their country house for the weekend. That helped a lot. It enabled her to walk with her head held high and to look about her with a cool, detached interest.

And when they finally made it inside

Eleanor realised it wasn't nearly as daunting a setting as she'd expected. Yes, the interior of the house was grand with its wood panelling and chandeliers. Yes, there was a sweeping staircase and huge fireplace — but she was relieved to see that the carpet looked a little worn in places and the house had a lived-in, comfortable feel about it. An underlying scent of beeswax polish set the seal on it — that was what her nana always used. Eleanor felt herself start to relax a little.

Soon she had a glass of wine in her hand and was being introduced to Fiona and Andrew's work colleagues, who seemed like a nice bunch. They were interested to meet and talk to her, having heard all about her from Fiona. They asked lots of questions about her work in the theatre and several congratulated her on the success of *Heavens Above!* They had obviously read the newspaper reviews — unlike her.

By the time she'd spotted some

familiar faces in the crowd she was starting to feel more at home. Betty McCardle was there, looking very glamorous despite her baby bump.

The man with her — presumably her husband (though with Betty you could never be sure) — was broodingly handsome but looked extremely uncomfortable in his dinner jacket. His muscles bulged against the sleeves as though they were trying to escape and Eleanor could see the shadow of a tattoo under the fine, white fabric of his shirt. He looked like he would rather be anywhere else on earth and was knocking back his pint at an alarming rate.

Craig Buchanan was there too, now with a walking stick to lean on rather than his crutches, and with Natalia at his side looking lovely in a simple black dress. They politely stopped to chat to Eleanor but it was obvious they wanted to be alone and enjoy the glittering occasion in each other's company.

She couldn't help smiling as she

watched them move off again. Natalia was at Craig's side, carrying their drinks and he kept turning back to make sure they hadn't got separated by the crowd. It was rather sweet.

Love was certainly in the air tonight. But where was her Prince Charming?

She looked around to see if she could find Mr and Mrs McIntyre — they might know where James was and what was going on, but there was no sign of them anywhere.

The two people she did see, who she would much rather not have seen, were the McBride sisters. What on earth were they doing here? she wondered.

Then she remembered what James had told her about local business people attending and realised that the lovely sisters, being joint owners of the village shop and post office, were probably a force to be reckoned within the local business community.

Eleanor couldn't help staring at them for a moment. Aggie had opted for a long, black dress, which with her bony frame and pale skin made her look even more witch-like than usual. Bridie, or rather Isobel, had managed to squeeze herself into a purple satin dress several sizes too small and looked like a ripe berry about to burst out of its skin. Eleanor quickly turned on her heel and walked away before they noticed her. With a bit of luck she might be able to avoid them all night in a crowd this size.

★ ★ ★

When it was time to go in to dinner and James still hadn't turned up, Eleanor started to get really annoyed. Being a bit late was one thing, but not turning up in time for the meal was another thing entirely. Unfortunately, as it was such a formal affair, just sitting down at any old table wasn't an option. There was a plan on an easel at the entrance to the dining room showing everyone which seat at which table they'd been allocated. That meant Eleanor couldn't simply join Fiona and Andrew and their noisy crowd from the hospital, who were getting rowdier by the minute.

Fiona mouthed 'sorry' at her as Andrew led her towards their table and Eleanor could see by the look on her friend's face that James would be in serious trouble when he finally turned up . . . if he ever did.

Worst of all, because James was some kind of guest of honour, Eleanor found herself at a table with Lord and Lady Ferguson and their other distinguished guests, with the seat on her right embarrassingly empty.

Thankfully the elderly American gentleman to her left and his wife took her under their wing. Mr and Mrs Harriman chatted happily about their home in Hartford, Connecticut, their three grown-up sons and their grand-children. This was their first trip to Scotland and they seemed to be enthralled by everything they had seen, from the castles and coastline to the knitwear and food.

Eleanor thoroughly enjoyed their company and was able to relax enough to enjoy the delicious food. There was a duck and green peppercorn pate to start with, followed by a joint of rare beef and pavlova or tiramisu for dessert.

But it was no thanks to James that she was able to enjoy herself. And because Mrs Harriman wouldn't allow any business talk at the table, it was only much later that Eleanor discovered she'd been sitting next to one of the wealthiest men in the world.

She had almost given up on James completely, but in the middle of the dessert course there was a commotion in the corner of the dining room nearest the door. The noise level, which had been fairly high already seemed to climb several decibels and people broke into a spontaneous round of applause.

Eleanor turned to find out what was going on and was stunned to see James standing there, looking unbelievably handsome and suave. The sight of him in a kilt took her breath away, but she barely had time to take in how devastatingly gorgeous he looked before she spotted the person walking in behind him. She sat, frozen in her seat. No wonder everyone was so excited. Not one, but two Hollywood legends gracing the Muirfield Ball!

She could see James's eyes scanning the room, even as he smiled, shook hands and politely responded to countless greetings. He was obviously looking for her, but she turned away to avoid meeting his eyes. She was just in time to see Lord Ferguson getting up from the table. Presumably he was going to greet James and his famous companion, Brandon Stone.

The next thing Eleanor knew, Brandon was at her side taking both her hands in his and pulling her to her feet so he could kiss her. There was another spontaneous round of applause, which he acknowledged with a slight wave.

Out of the corner of her eye Eleanor saw James watching, an unreadable expression on his face. In a moment the look was gone, to be replaced by his professional Hollywood smile as he accompanied Lord Ferguson to a raised dais with a podium on it. She quickly sat back down and to her annoyance Brandon joined her, taking the seat reserved for James.

'You don't mind, do you?' he asked, with his trademark lopsided smile.

Eleanor had no choice but to murmur politely, 'Not at all,' through gritted teeth. She could have screamed with frustration. Despite the fact that James was inexcusably late — though the reason for that was obvious and was sitting right next to her — she just wanted to be with him. She wanted to talk to him, laugh with him and dance all night. What she didn't want was to be sitting next to a man she'd sincerely hoped never to. see again.

★   ★   ★

Lord Ferguson tapped the microphone and his voice rang out through the room.

'Ladies and gentlemen,' he began, loudly clearing his throat. When the noise died down he carried on, 'I'd like to thank you all for joining me this evening. My wife and I are delighted to welcome you to our home for the two hundred and forty-second annual ball to be held here at Muirfield House.'

His final words were almost drowned out by claps and cheers, whistles and stamping of feet.

'As you all know, while the Muirfield Ball is primarily a social occasion we also use it as an opportunity to raise funds for various charitable causes. Tonight, the money raised from our auction will be going to Wishes Do Come True, the children's cancer charity. So I hope you'll all give very generously.

'Now it's time for me to shut up — as I'm sure you'll all be very pleased to hear — and to hand over to a man who needs no introduction. Ladies and gentlemen, I give you our very own local hero, Mr James McIntyre.'

The room erupted with applause and James stepped up to the microphone.

'Thank you, Lord Ferguson. And a very big thank you to everyone for such a warm welcome, especially as I'm inexcusably late.' There was laughter from the audience. He looked directly at Eleanor. 'My date for the evening will probably never forgive me. But I'm hoping.the rest of you will, seeing as I've brought along a special guest — Mr Brandon Stone.'

There was more applause and cheers from the crowd.

'He's come directly from London to join us tonight, where — as I'm sure you all know — he's currently starring in the hit show *Heavens Above!* directed by the supremely talented Eleanor Christie.'

Brandon stood and pulled Eleanor to her feet again, raising his empty glass to her in a silent toast. Everyone joined in.

'Will you please stop doing that?' she asked furiously out of the corner of her mouth as they sat back down again.

'I knew it — you haven't forgiven me,' he replied, looking crestfallen. 'That's why I made James bring me here tonight. I've been looking everywhere for you, Eleanor. I wanted to apologise.'

Eleanor turned and looked at him properly for the first time. For once Brandon wasn't drunk and he wasn't posturing; he looked genuinely upset and sincerely apologetic.

'Go on, then,' she said.

He smiled, less confidently this time.

'I know I was a nightmare during rehearsals and made a complete hash of the opening night. But I'm truly sorry. And seeing as how everything has turned out just fine — despite me — don't you think you could let bygones be bygones?'

Eleanor smiled in spite of herself. She'd never had a Hollywood heart-throb grovelling to her before and she was only human after all.

'Yes, Brandon, I think I could. Apology accepted,' she replied and meant it.

Brandon gave a sigh and seemed to relax.

'Oh — I nearly forgot, I wanted to return this to you as well.' He slid his hand into his inside jacket pocket and produced her mobile phone, complete with its sparkly case. 'You left it at the theatre,' he explained. 'I've charged it for you.'

Somewhere between his hand and hers, the phone slipped. It ended up on the floor, slightly under the table so Brandon pushed back his chair and crawled around on the floor to retrieve it. Still down on one knee, he passed it up to Eleanor.

'Keep a tight hold of it this time,' he said. 'I may well not be around to return it the next time you lose it!'

He passed the phone up to her with a smile, which Eleanor returned.

'I promise,' she said, 'and thank you.'

She took the phone from him and sat with it on her lap so she could quickly flip through the reams of messages and missed calls in case she'd missed anything vital.

A waiter appeared with wine and tried to fill Brandon's glass. He covered it with his hand.

'No thanks, man. But I wouldn't mind something to eat if there's any leftovers in the kitchen,' he said winking.

The waiter looked torn between horror at the idea of serving leftover food, and delight at being treated so familiarly by a famous film star. Delight triumphed.

'I'll see what I can do, sir,' he replied, melting unobtrusively into the background.

Brandon reached for the jug of iced water on the table and filled his wine glass. Eleanor decided to join him. She'd only had one glass of wine — just to settle her nerves when she arrived — and had then quickly reverted to fruit juice, remembering Flona's warning about the need to pace herself.

When the waiter returned moments later with a plate piled high with piping hot food Brandon thanked him profusely and started to tuck in. Between mouthfuls and, under cover of the auction, which was now in full swing, he carried on talking to Eleanor.

'I can't thank you enough for giving me my big break in the theatre. I much prefer it to the movies, you know,' he told her confidentially.

'You do?' Eleanor asked, trying to keep the disbelief out of her voice.

'Absolutely! I've always found it really difficult to act with a camera and boom shoved in my face. Make-up and wardrobe are always hovering around too, which makes me nervous. It's so much easier on the stage, where you can stay totally immersed in the role right up until the interval. And I'm much happier doing comedy.'

He lowered his voice, so she had to lean in to hear what he was saying.

'I've cut out the drinking completely and I'm totally on the wagon now. I just wasn't cut out play the handsome hero — not like James.'

Eleanor looked up at the podium. James was taking bids for the latest item in the auction, but he seemed to feel her gaze on him. He looked up and caught her eye.

She smiled. After that he seemed to throw himself into his role with more gusto and soon had everyone laughing with his impromptu comments about the next lot and the bidders.

'I don't know how he does that,' Brandon commented.

'Does what?' Eleanor asked.

'What he's doing now — improvising. I was never any good at improv. If someone hands me the lines I can deliver them, but I would never be able to make them up by myself.'

Brandon spent the rest of the auction singing James's praises to Eleanor and taking all the blame for their late arrival. He really didn't need to, as she'd already forgiven James completely, but she found his friend's efforts very endearing. Maybe she'd misread Brandon all along.

By the time the final lot came up they were getting along famously.

James's sangfroid seemed to desert him slightly when he announced the final item, which turned out to be a dinner date — with him.

Eleanor watched in a mixture of annoyance and amusement as first one wealthy woman, then another offered silly amounts of money for an evening with James. She was just wishing she had the money to join in with the bidding, when it occurred to her that she didn't need to. She'd already spent lots of evenings with James, and she'd be spending the rest of this one with him too when the auction was over.

She was feeling justifiably smug and really starting to look forward to the dancing when a strident voice with an unmistakable Texan twang called out from the back of the room.

'I'll give you ten thousand dollars, darlin'!'

There were gasps from the audience and everyone turned to see who had made such an extravagant bid. There, at the back of the room making one of the most spectacular entrances Eleanor had ever seen, was the American actress Katie Jayne Mitchell. She was wearing a fire-engine-red dress that would have made Liz Hurley blush and looking every inch the Hollywood siren.

19

After that everything seemed to happen at once, but in excruciatingly slow motion.

First the dining room erupted with sound, then Katie Jayne sashayed slowly towards the podium, giving everyone plenty of time to admire her swaying hips. Not that she had much in the way of hips, Eleanor noted, just hipbones and an ironing-board flat stomach.

But as though to make up for the lack of curves below she had the most enormous bust, which looked as though it might escape from the confines of that little red dress at any moment. Most of the men in the audience were probably hoping it would.

'Ah'v come to collect ma prize,' Katie Jayne said breathily into the microphone in a very Marilyn Monroe-esque

291

way. She then turned, pulled James towards her by the lapels on his dinner jacket and kissed him.

There was cheering and wolf whistles and lots of heckling from the men in the audience, shouting comments about some men having all the luck. But Eleanor didn't think James looked as though he felt lucky, in fact he looked completely stunned.

Eleanor hadn't been able to drag her eyes away from the car crash happening in front of her, so she'd seen James turning to stone as Katie Jayne approached. And afterwards — for a moment so brief Eleanor wasn't sure she whether she'd imagined it or not — she thought she saw a look of absolute fury. But then his Hollywood mask had dropped firmly back into place.

'I don't think that's quite my shade, Katie Jayne,' he said into the microphone, playing to the audience as he wiped her scarlet lipstick from his mouth with the back of his hand.

Everyone laughed and Lord Ferguson made a beeline for the podium. He thanked James for his sterling work on the auction, but all the time his eyes were fixed on Katie Jayne. Then he announced that dancing would begin in the ballroom shortly and recommended everyone put their best foot forward for the Scottish reels, nearly forgetting to mention the disco and casino in the marquees.

While everyone finished their coffees and gathered their belongings, he tried to engage Katie Jayne in conversation but she had threaded her arm through James's and was sticking to his side like a burr.

Chairs were pushed back from tables and people started to get up and leave the dining room. Eleanor sat frozen in her seat, her eyes on James and Katie Jayne.

Before she had a chance to gather herself together and move, she became aware of someone standing beside her chair. She turned and looked up into the gaunt, almost skeletal face of Aggie McBride.

'That's her,' Aggie said, unnecessarily. 'That's the American actress we told you about.'

'We did try to warn you,' Bridie added, from her other side. She was obviously trying to sound sympathetic but only managing triumphant.

Eleanor was trapped. With one sister on either side of her there was nowhere to go. Brandon. came unexpectedly to her rescue.

'Excuse us, ladies,' he said, getting to his feet and holding out his hand to Eleanor. 'We've got some dancing to do.'

As she took his arm and gratefully walked away she couldn't help overhearing Aggie's final comment.

'Now she'll find out what it was like for the local girls who got pushed to one side when she turned up. I wonder how she'll like it?'

★　★　★

'What exactly is a reel?' Brandon asked, as they followed the crowd heading to the ballroom.

Eleanor gave a rather shaky laugh and explained it was a type of dance that mainly involved swinging your partner round a lot.

'Sounds like fun,' Brandon said. 'Care to show me how it's done?'

Eleanor desperately wanted to leave. The evening, which had been disappointing from the start, was becoming a complete nightmare. But pride stopped her from scuttling away the minute Katie Jayne appeared. That and the thought of Aggie and Bridie, who would have a field day if she did.

But no way could she compete with the woman who'd recently been voted one of the sexiest women in the world, and frankly she wasn't even going to try. If James preferred Katie Jayne to her — and even she had to admit he'd be mad not to — then so be it. She wasn't going to let him know her heart was breaking.

She'd stay for the first round of dancing and gracefully bow out before the supper break. But there was no way she was going to spend the next couple of hours watching the gorgeous American actress pawing at James. That was more than flesh and blood could stand. No, instead she'd make every woman in the place — and hopefully James too — jealous, as she twirled the night away in the arms of one of the handsomest men at the ball. That would show them all!

'I'd be delighted,' she said and she meant it. Brandon Stone might not be the Prince Charming she'd been hoping for, but he'd have to do.

'Good girl,' Brandon said encouragingly. 'Chin up.' And he gave her arm a gentle squeeze as they walked into the ballroom.

*   *   *

The atmosphere in Muirfield House was electric. The good citizens of

Tullymuir didn't know what had hit them. Having not one, not two, but three Hollywood movie stars in their midst was too much for them.

Everyone was skittish and on edge. The laughter was too loud, the dancing too wild. Eleanor saw a number of couples arguing and several women on the verge of tears.

Well, she definitely wasn't going to join them. If there was one thing she'd learned as an actress, it was how to put on a good performance no matter how she was feeling. She could fall apart later when she got back to her grandparents' house but for now, she had to keep her emotions firmly under control. Dancing with Brandon would be a good distraction.

Eleanor pulled herself together and found she was actually able to enjoy her attempts to teach Brandon the basics of a reel. She was aware of lots of envious female eyes turned in her direction. But she couldn't enjoy the attention — not when she kept catching a flash of red out of the corner of her eye as Katie Jayne moved about the room.

Eleanor didn't turn and look properly. She didn't want to see James talking to Katie Jayne and laughing. It would make all the time they'd spent together over the past few weeks seem empty and hollow.

And she definitely didn't want to see him smiling at Katie Jayne in the way she'd been so sure he reserved for her alone: his genuine, slightly shy smile, the one that lit up his eyes, not the fake Hollywood one he could turn on and off like a light switch.

She did her best to laugh and flirt with Brandon and felt as though she was putting on quite a convincing performance. Meanwhile, Brandon kept offering to draw Katie Jayne off, so that she and James could dance together.

'I feel really bad,' he said, when they took a break from the dancing to catch their breath. 'If I hadn't come up here as soon as James told me you were staying with your grandparents in

Tullymuir, none of this would have happened. It was collecting me from the airport, then sorting me out with something suitable to wear that made James late. I'm the reason he phoned your grandparents and left a message saying he'd meet you here. The least I can do is try to run interference.'

'Thanks, Brandon, but I'm not sure I really want to talk to James right now,' Eleanor said. She'd just seen him twirling Katie Jayne Mitchell around the room and he certainly hadn't looked unhappy about it.

'I'm sure this is all just a misunderstanding, Eleanor. James did nothing but talk about you all afternoon,' Brandon said, staunchly defending his friend. 'Katie Jayne is just his co-star in the next movie he's making.'

'She's his what?' she demanded, turning to look Brandon in the face before her eyes were drawn back to the dancers.

'His co-star,' he repeated falteringly. 'He must have forgotten to mention that when I was helping him learn his lines,' she said acidly.

'I'm sure there's nothing more to it than that,' Brandon ploughed on.

'Oh really?' Eleanor asked, watching them do a particularly fancy twirl, which ended with Katie Jayne bending over backwards supported by James's arm. When he helped her back up they laughed and Katie Jayne entwined her arms around James's neck. The look she gave him could have scorched the paintwork off Eleanor's new car. The air around them seemed to sizzle and men's eyes were drawn to Katie Jayne like moths to a flame.

'I wish I could believe you.'

'She's really not a very nice person, you know,' Brandon carried on valiantly, doing his best to reassure her.

'I can well believe it, but I've noticed men don't always seem to bother too much about that. A lot of them seem to go by looks rather than personality.'

'Sure, some do, but not all men and definitely not James,' Brandon soldiered on. 'He's a genuinely nice guy — one of the nicest people I've ever met.'

'I must admit, that's what I thought,' Eleanor said wistfully.

'Then give him the benefit of the doubt. I'll see if I can get Katie Jayne to dance with me for a while so you two can make things up,' he added persuasively.

* * *

Which was why, a few moments later Eleanor found herself watching Brandon cross the dance floor and tap James lightly on the shoulder.

Eleanor was too far away to hear what they were saying, but their body language said it all. Even from the side lines Eleanor could see the two men squaring up to each other as though they were about to have a fight, James standing in front of Katie Jayne to block her from Brandon. He obviously had no intention of giving up his partner.

Eleanor didn't wait to see any more.

If they chose to have a punch-up on the dance floor, that was up to them. But the fact that James was so reluctant to let Katie Jayne go for even a moment, made her heart ache.

She turned on her heel and left the ballroom. Her first impulse was to run, to take off her shoes — which were killing her — pick up the hem of her long dress and run. Instead, she made her way to an upstairs bathroom that had been designated as one of the ladies' loos and shut herself in there in privacy for a while.

After she'd managed to pull herself together, she re-did her make up at the mirror and spritzed on her favourite perfume. With her war paint on and a haze of Opium round her head, she went in search of Fiona.

It didn't take long to find her, mainly because her friend was searching for her too. They met on the stairs and Fiona linked arms with her.

'Let's go for a wander,' Fiona suggested.

Eleanor nodded, mute with misery.

Fiona led her downstairs through a maze of corridors until they had left all the partygoers behind and even the music was slightly muffled by all the heavy doors they'd passed through.

'I think I'm going to head home,' Eleanor said, when they were finally alone. 'The evening isn't turning out the way I'd imagined it.'

'No — I can see that,' Fiona said, a look of sympathy in her eyes.

'In fact, apart from getting ready at your house earlier, it's been a total disaster! From the moment you got that phone call from Nana, it all seems to have gone wrong.'

'I don't understand what's going on,' Fiona said. 'What the hell is James playing at?'

'I've no idea and I don't much care,' Eleanor said, stifling a sob. 'No — that's not true. I do care. A lot. But so much has happened so quickly I can't get my head around it.

'First James says not to pick him up

because he's running late, then he turns up with Brandon Stone, then Katie Jayne Mitchell appears and is all over him like a rash. All it needs is for him to propose to her and it'll put the tin lid on what has been the worst night of my life!'

Fiona tried to give her friend a hug.

'Don't!' Eleanor burst out, taking a step away from her. 'If you hug me or give me any sympathy at all, I'll break down completely and I'm determined to leave with my head held high. Besides, my feet are killing me and I just want to go home.'

'Well, if your feet are killing you, there's noway round it — you'd better go now, this minute,' Fiona said, gently teasing her. 'Why don't you just take your shoes off? I'm sure you won't be the only one.'

Eleanor took her advice and stood wriggling her newly-released toes on the carpet.

'Bliss!' she muttered and stooped to pick up the offending footwear. 'What a shame, they're so gorgeous and sparkly too.'

'Never mind the damn shoes,' Fiona said. 'Will you be OK to drive yourself home or would you like me to find Andrew and we'll all go together?'

'Thanks, Fiona, but I'd much rather you stayed. I really don't want to make a big fuss, and it'll be much easier for me to slip away unnoticed if I'm on my own. You guys stay on and enjoy your evening to the full. Remember, it's your work do, too — you can't just skip out on all your colleagues.'

Fiona hesitated, looking uncertain.

'And I've only drunk one glass of wine all night,' Eleanor added. 'It was a very long time ago now, so I can assure you, I'll be perfectly safe to drive.'

'Well, if you're sure . . . '

At last Eleanor was free to escape. She was standing at the front door trying to force her reluctant feet back into her shoes when she heard James calling her name. She'd only managed to get one shoe on, but when she turned and saw him standing at the top of the grand staircase with Katie Jayne, she tore it back off again so she could make a quicker getaway.

She raced down the outside steps, the shock of the icy-cold stone making her drop one of the shoes she was carrying. But she didn't care — she wouldn't be wearing them again in a hurry. Or at all.

As she climbed into her car, the clock in the stable yard chimed midnight. Eleanor would have laughed at the irony of it all if she hadn't been feeling so miserable. Her life seemed to be turning into a hideously warped version of the Cinderella story.

She sped down the drive, narrowly missing several lanterns and heedless of potholes, watching in the rear view mirror as the sky behind her lit up with colourful fireworks.

She was too far away to see a figure on the steps, stooping to pick something up.

20

James was desperate to talk to Eleanor. He rang and rang all morning. The first half dozen times the phone was answered, but always by Janet. And after that there was no ring tone, just silence, as though the phone had been unplugged.

He drove over instead. But he'd hardly climbed off Bessie before Eleanor's grandfather intercepted him in the driveway.

'I'm sorry, lad, but she doesn't want to see you,' Davy said mendaciously.

'If I could just speak to her, try to explain . . . '

'Why don't you leave it a bit until everyone's calmed down?' the older man suggested.

'But . . . '

If this had been one of his movies James would have broken down the front door to get to the woman he loved. But this was real life. Good manners prevented him from barging past a neighbour and vandalising his property.

All he could do was give a curt nod and turn on his heel. Sometimes he wished real life was more like the movies.

He drove away feeling angry and frustrated. If only Eleanor's grandparents would stop behaving like a pair of guard dogs and let him speak to her, he was sure he could straighten everything out.

The drive home calmed him down and allowed common sense to filter through the raw emotion he was feeling.

They could only stop him from seeing her for so long. The first performance of the pantomime was tomorrow night. The technical rehearsal for sound and lighting had been a week ago, and the dress rehearsal the day before the ball. One way or another, he'd be seeing Eleanor soon — if not today, then definitely tomorrow at the pre-show walk-through.

He could see now that it had been a mistake not to mention his fears about Katie Jayne to her. But when he'd last spoken to his agent, Katie Jayne Mitchell had only been one of three actresses auditioning to play opposite him in his next movie. Nothing had been decided.

He gathered from his agent — whom he'd called that morning and woken up, as it was the middle of the night back in the States — that was still the case. Typically, Katie Jayne had jumped the gun. Maybe she was hoping that if their names were romantically linked in real life it might help her land the role?

But James was determined that was never going to happen. So he out-manoeuvred her, making it very clear to his agent that he wasn't prepared to do the movie at all if Katie Jayne was cast opposite him.

It wasn't often James played the diva,

it really wasn't his style, but he knew it was his name the studio was relying on to attract audiences. After the string of successes he'd had, he was in a very strong position and he'd use that or whatever else it took to save his love life.

Katie Jayne had already done her best to scupper his blossoming romance with Eleanor by gate-crashing the ball. If she ended up as his co-star he was pretty sure it would put an end to it completely. And he wasn't about to let that happen.

The hours dragged. James felt as though he was losing his mind. Each time he looked at his watch, the hands hardly seemed to have moved at all. The day stretched endlessly in front of him, the long hours before he would see Eleanor again seeming interminable.

★   ★   ★

Eleanor wanted time to stand still. She didn't know how she was going to get through tomorrow's performance, let alone two nights in a row.

But she had no choice: the tickets for both the Friday and Saturday night had sold out completely. Besides, the rest of the cast were ready and eager — just as she, too, had been before the Muirfield Ball. And on top of that, she'd promised her grandparents she would help save *Cinderella* and the Tullymuir Dramatic Society, so she would have to go through with it.

She just didn't know how. How was she going to face James? How was she going to stand on the stage beside him, say her lines, dance with him, hold his hand when they bowed at the end? How was she going to do all that, knowing he didn't love her after all?

She was going to have to put on the performance of a lifetime, that was how! And she only had a day to get her act together and her head in the right place to be able to pull it off. She looked at her watch, horrified to find

311

that several precious hours had flown by without her realising.

* ★ *

James was standing outside the village hall when Eleanor arrived. They were both far too early; Eleanor because she had the key to open up, and James because he was determined to speak to her before the others arrived.

'We need to talk,' he said, launching head first into it.

Eleanor fumbled with the key in the lock.

'I'm not sure this is the best time, James,' she answered calmly. 'We've got a show to do in a couple of hours and we both need to be concentrating on that.'

'We're more important than a pantomime,' he objected, following her into the hall.

'Not to all the people who've paid good money for their tickets and are expecting to be entertained,' she pointed out.

'OK, so for their benefit then, we need to sort this out before we step on that stage. Come on, Eleanor,' he pleaded, 'it won't be long until the others arrive — at least hear me out.'

'All right,' Eleanor said. 'I'm listening.'

'I can explain everything,' James began. 'If you give me a chance.'

'Go on then,' she said, folding her arms across her chest.

'You're a tough audience,' he joked, trying unsuccessfully to raise a smile. 'Look, I know I behaved like an idiot at the ball, but there was a reason for that.'

Eleanor raised a sceptical eyebrow but let him continue.

'I knew — I'd known for a while — that Brandon was trying to find you. And when I told him you were here in Tullymuir he hopped straight on a plane and flew up, which was worrying as I thought he might be in love with you himself.'

Eleanor's ears pricked up at that

point. Did that mean James was in love with her? She allowed herself a flicker of hope.

'Anyway, as soon as he arrived I told him how I feel about you.'

'And how exactly do you feel about me, James McIntyre?'

'That's what I've been trying to tell you,' he said, taking her hand. 'I love you, Eleanor Christie. That's why I behaved like a fool at the ball.'

Eleanor met James's eye for the first time.

'You do?' she asked, trying hard not to grin.

'Yes! So when I saw Brandon get down on one knee and propose to you at the dinner table, I just freaked out. I couldn't believe my best buddy had stabbed me in the back like that.'

'What on earth are you talking about?' Eleanor asked. 'Brandon didn't propose to me!'

'I know that now,' James continued. 'He explained about dropping your phone. But that's not what it looked like. All I saw was him getting down on one knee, handing you something and you smiling at him. I think it was your smile that pushed me over the edge — it looked exactly as though you'd said yes.

'So you'll understand that I was seeing red long before Katie Jayne turned up in that ridiculous dress. Anyway, I was so angry and jealous that I ended up behaving like a prize idiot. When Katie Jayne arrived out of the blue, I flirted with her outrageously in the hopes of making you jealous.'

'Well, it worked. And that's why I was dancing with Brandon, too,' Eleanor admitted. 'So why did you stop him dancing with Katie Jayne when he tried to draw her off?'

'I didn't know that's what he was doing! He explained it all afterwards, but at the time I thought he was deliberately goading me. As if it wasn't enough, him stealing a march on me with you, he was coming to take away my dance partner too.'

'Stealing a march on you?' Eleanor asked, her heart thumping in her chest. 'Does that mean . . .'

'Er yes, it does,' James admitted. 'I love you and I want us to be together, always.'

He took her in his arms and kissed her hungrily.

'I've missed you so much,' he said fervently when they came up for air. 'I didn't know if I'd ever get to hold you again.' His voice broke on the words. 'Look — this isn't how I was planning on proposing to you. I was going to buy a huge rock to put on your finger, take you somewhere special and go down on one knee. But after thinking I'd lost you, I can't wait any longer.'

Eleanor looked at him in disbelief.

'I know the prop room in Tullymuir village hall isn't the most romantic place,' he said with a wry smile, 'but, Ella . . . will you marry me?'

Eleanor grinned.

'Actually I think it's the perfect place for a couple of actors to get engaged.'

'Is that a 'yes'?' James asked tensely.

'It most certainly is!' Eleanor said, her eyes sparkling with happiness.

'I don't have a ring to give you — just this,' he said, producing one of the sparkly shoes she'd worn to the ball from his jacket pocket.

When the rest of the cast started arriving shortly afterwards they found Cinderella and Prince Charming in each other's arms.

'Oi, cut it out, now, you two,' Tommy said. 'You've got to wait until the end for that!'

* * *

Afterwards it was always held by the residents of Tullymuir that James McIntyre and Eleanor Christie gave the performances of their lives that night. Their love lit up the stage and filled the hall with magic.

And when they kissed at the end — which was, it had to be said, not part of the original script — there was not a

317

single dry eye in the house.

Everywhere eyes sparkled with tears of joy and Eleanor could have sworn she even saw Aggie and Bridie sniffing into their handkerchiefs. Every single member of the audience and cast went home feeling uplifted, with a spring in their step and hope in their hearts.

★   ★   ★

'So — that's that, then,' Eleanor said when the Saturday night performance was over. Like most actors, she always felt rather flat when the show ended. 'All that hard work and it's over in two nights flat.'

'But just think how much everyone enjoyed themselves,' James said, wrapping his arms around her. 'My mum and dad came along to see the show last night and they haven't stopped talking about it since. Oh — and by the way, they've gone away now to visit my brother for the weekend . . . '

'Oh?' Eleanor said, her heart starting

to thump with anticipation.

'You obviously need a bit of cheering up, and I think I know what might do the trick,' he continued.

Eleanor raised an eyebrow.

'Fancy coming home and making . . . hot chocolate with me?'

Eleanor gave a deliciously slow smile.

'Ooh, yes please!' she said.

We do hope that you have enjoyed reading this large print book.

Did you know that all of our titles are available for purchase?

We publish a wide range of high quality large print books including:
Romances, Mysteries, Classics
General Fiction
Non Fiction and Westerns

Special interest titles available in large print are:
The Little Oxford Dictionary
Music Book, Song Book
Hymn Book, Service Book

Also available from us courtesy of Oxford University Press:
Young Readers' Dictionary
(large print edition)
Young Readers' Thesaurus
(large print edition)

For further information or a free brochure, please contact us at:
Ulverscroft Large Print Books Ltd.,
The Green, Bradgate Road, Anstey,
Leicester, LE7 7FU, England.
Tel: (00 44) **0116 236 4325**
Fax: (00 44) **0116 234 0205**

MEDITERRANEAN MYSTERY

Evelyn Orange

Leda unexpectedly finds herself companion to her great aunt on a Mediterranean cruise. Assuming it will be a boring holiday with a crowd of elderly people, her horizons change as she explores the ports of call, and discovers that Aunt Ronnie is lively company. There's also a handsome ship's officer who seems to be attracted to Leda, plus intriguing fellow passenger Nick, who's hiding something. Added into the mix is a mystery on the ship — which becomes a voyage with unforeseen consequences . . .

FIRESTORM

Alan C. Williams

1973: Debra Winters has started a new life for herself as a teacher in a small Australian outback town. Given the responsibility of updating the school's fire protocol, she is thrown together with volunteer firefighter Robbie Sanderson, and there's a spark of attraction between them. Meanwhile, things are heating up: it's bushfire season, and there's an arsonist on the loose. Debra and Robbie find themselves in danger. Will their relationship flicker out — or will they set each other's worlds alight?